Local gossip painted Sam Frazier as a black sheep. Wild as a mustang.

Molly herself sometimes felt insulted by the rugged rancher's harsh, unsmiling manner.

But then there was the look in his eyes—eyes the color of clear, dark molasses—when he gazed at motherless little Lass....

In those intense depths, Molly saw the love Sam had for his infant daughter. A fierce, protective love that was utterly sweet and filled with such tenderness, it brought a lump to her throat.

The way it did now.

For that look, Molly could forgive Sam Frazier anything.

Why, at times, she even dreamed he'd look at *her* that way....

Dear Reader,

Spring is just beginning in the month of April for Special Edition!

Award-winning author Laurie Paige presents our THAT'S MY BABY! title for the month, *Molly Darling*. Take one ranching single dad, a proper schoolteacher and an irresistible baby girl, and romance is sure to follow. Don't miss this wonderful story that is sure to melt your heart!

Passions are running high when *New York Times* bestselling author Nora Roberts pits a charming ladies' man against his match—this MacKade brother just doesn't know what hit him in *The Fall of Shane MacKade*, the fourth book in Nora's series, THE MACKADE BROTHERS. Trisha Alexander's new series of weddings and babies, THREE BRIDES AND A BABY, begins this month with *A Bride for Luke*. And Joan Elliott Pickart's THE BABY BET series continues in April with *The Father of Her Child*. Rounding out the month is Jennifer Mikels with the tender *Expecting: Baby*, and Judith Yates's warm family tale, *A Will and a Wedding*.

A whole season of love and romance has just begun from Special Edition! I hope you enjoy each and every story to come!

Sincerely,

Tara Gavin
Senior Editor

Please address questions and book requests to:
Silhouette Reader Service
U.S.: 3010 Walden Ave., P.O. Box 1325, Buffalo, NY 14269
Canadian: P.O. Box 609, Fort Erie, Ont. L2A 5X3

LAURIE PAIGE

MOLLY DARLING

Published by Silhouette Books
America's Publisher of Contemporary Romance

To Mary-Theresa Hussey

 SILHOUETTE BOOKS

ISBN 0-373-24021-X

MOLLY DARLING

Printed in U.S.A.

Books by Laurie Paige

LAURIE PAIGE

was recently presented with the *Affaire de Coeur* Readers' Choice Silver Pen Award for Favorite Contemporary Author. In addition, she was a 1994 Romance Writers of America RITA finalist for Best Traditional Romance for her book *Sally's Beau*. She reports romance is blooming in her part of Northern California. With the birth of a second grandson, she finds herself madly in love with three wonderful males—"all hero material." So far, her husband hasn't complained about the other men in her life.

Dear Reader,

Picture one spinsterish heroine, a nursery-school teacher with her own successful business, an impeccable reputation and the esteem of the whole community. Why would she up and marry one growly hero with an attitude, a reputation as a "black sheep" and a six-month-old daughter to raise?

I don't know about you, but it does something to me to see a man with a baby, his touch gentle, maybe a bit unsure, as he holds the infant in his arms. I go all melty inside. Recently, flying home from Chicago, I listened to the man behind me on the plane playing cards with his very young daughter. He was funny and charming, his heart obviously wrapped around her little finger. It was a delightful trip. I smiled all the way home....

Sincerely,

Laurie Paige

Chapter One

Molly Clelland flicked the curtain aside and frowned at the empty driveway. Sam Frazier was late. Again.

She studied the clouds. Thunderheads clashed like medieval knights decked out in gray plumes as they raced over Roswell, twelve miles west of her, and charged across the winter sky.

The huge cloud masses had hovered over the landscape all day, ominous and dreary, threatening anyone who ventured out. She sighed. She really wanted to get home before it rained for the third day in a row.

Turning from the window, she put the dust cloth away and finished straightening the basement room of the church, then stretched and yawned. It had been a long day.

She'd opened the nursery school at seven that morning and had hardly sat down a moment since then.

By now—six-thirty at night—she should have been safe at home, snug in the adobe cottage across the street from the church, sipping a cup of hot tea and catching up on the world news on television. The cats were probably howling for their supper.

Where the heck was Sam Frazier?

He knew the rules. He should. She'd had to remind him of them often enough during the past four months. Worry wound its way through the irritation as thunder pealed overhead.

Torrential rains had fallen all that week. Here in the southeastern corner of New Mexico, they occasionally got the edge of a fierce storm blowing in from the Gulf of Mexico.

Llano Estacado. The Staked Plain. A plateau of desert hues and formations with mountain peaks thrusting upward as if the land sought the caress of the sky. However, this land, beautiful as it was, could be treacherous. A dry wash could become a raging river without warning.

She'd fallen in love with New Mexico ten years ago when she'd arrived as a summer teaching volunteer in a federal program—the proverbial do-gooder—and had vowed to stay.

So here she was at thirty-two, spinning out her modest dreams in this land of enchantment with her own nursery school and a cozy little house where she lived with two cats.

The proverbial spinster.

Her parents called her their "changeling." She was unlike the rest of her family. Where they were laughing and witty, she was serious, given to lectures on nutrition, the value of hard work and the cultivation of sober habits. She found them fascinating but exhausting. They found her prim but amusing.

A gurgle interrupted her thoughts. She crossed to the crib in the corner and peered down at the six-month-old baby.

Lass Frazier let go of the bright booties covering her feet and grinned up at Molly, waving her arms in the air and making her little sounds of welcome.

"Hello, darling," Molly murmured. "Do you need a change?"

Lecturing about the weather, the lateness of the hour and the thoughtlessness of men, she put a fresh diaper on the tiny girl and lifted the child into her arms.

Lass touched Molly's lips, then her nose, then clutched a handful of hair and tried to taste it.

Molly gently tugged the lock from the child's hold and gave her a rabbit teething ring to chew on.

"Where is your father?" she asked.

Lass gave her a big grin, then clicked her tongue against the roof of her mouth several times, evidently liking the sound, while Molly walked to the window and peered outside again.

The church was built on the side of a hill, its front door opening on a circular driveway. The nursery was accessible from a winding lane that led down the hill and behind the building. A stand of junipers interrupted the rocky ground that sloped off toward a dry wash, now running in muddy torrents.

Headlights appeared on the lane. A truck slowed and stopped at the end of the sidewalk leading to the basement door. The driver jumped out and strode up the walkway with his usual long-legged stride and preoccupied air.

He fascinated her, this silent, unsmiling man with a forebidding presence. Like the land, he had an aura of vastness, of limitless distances and a toughness that had to do with survival and determination and other facets of being that she couldn't define.

The local gossip painted him black. While still a teenager, he'd been caught rustling cattle from his own family's ranch. The charges had been dropped, but where there was smoke...

After a significant look, the storyteller would continue. The Frazier boy had fought constantly with his stepfather...had left home as soon as he got out of high school...had been a trial to his poor mother, bless her soul. Yes, he was a bad one, that Sam Frazier. As wild as a mustang, you know.

Molly thought of what she knew of Sam Frazier. One, he was a man, not a boy. His boyhood had disappeared long ago. Two, he took better care of his daughter than many mothers she'd known.

She fixed a smile on her face when the door opened, then closed behind him. He filled the room, bringing the fresh scent of the outdoors with him. Sam Frazier wasn't a brawny man, nor unusually tall, but he dominated the space around him. When he removed his hat, drops of water fell to the floor.

"Good evening. Looks like it's raining out your way," she said, determined to be pleasant. Ill manners didn't win friends or solve problems. "Were the roads bad?"

He answered her greeting with a nod. "Yes, it's raining. The roads aren't bad yet. I had a cow that was down with a calf," he explained his tardiness.

It was as close to an apology as she was going to get from him. She instinctively knew he was a man who didn't like having to explain himself to others, nor was he given to small talk. In four months of twice daily meetings, five days a week, they hadn't exchanged more than the most cursory of comments, and not one of them personal.

For a second, she tried to think of something personal he might say to her, then gave up when nothing came to mind except a dash of poetry—*come be my love*. She frowned at her musing.

He raked a hand through his black, curly hair while his eyes, the color of dark, clear molasses, fastened on his daughter as if to make certain she'd made it through the day without mishap.

Molly sometimes felt insulted by his manner. However, she was sure it was an unconscious gesture on his part. And there was the look in his eyes when he gazed at Lass.

Sometimes in those intense depths, in a flash before he hid his feelings, she saw the love he had for his daughter—a fierce, protective love that was utterly sweet and filled with such tenderness, it brought a lump to her throat.

The way it did now.

For that look, she could forgive him anything. At times, she even dreamed he'd look at her that way someday.

Mentally shaking her head at her extravagant fantasies, she nodded toward the clock. "Lass just woke up. I think she's hungry. Perhaps we should feed her before you make the trip back to your place?"

He paused after picking up the bag of Lass's belongings and considered the suggestion as if it were of world importance.

Molly had to smile. Here was a person who evidently took life even more seriously than she did. Her parents would marvel over that.

"Would you like to go out to dinner?" he asked.

She tried to figure out what he'd said. It sounded as if he'd invited her out to dinner. She must have misunderstood.

"I beg your pardon?" She removed a tendril of her hair from Lass's fist and substituted a rattle.

Lass shook the rattle, then settled happily to chewing on the bright red handle.

"It's late. I've kept you from your supper. I thought we could go somewhere and eat."

"Oh." Her heart kicked up a bit before common sense reasserted itself. "That's all right. You don't have to do that. Lass was a perfect angel. I didn't mind keeping her."

He gave her an impatient frown. "I'm as hungry as a bear. I've been working since before dawn, and I'd like to sit down and relax a bit."

"Oh." She cleared her throat. "Well, of course. That would be nice." She peered down at her slacks and blouse, which were wrinkled from a day of tending children under four years of age. "I'd better stop by the house and change."

"You'll do," he said, giving her an impersonal once-over with his quick, restless gaze.

After shifting Lass to one side, Molly picked her purse and coat up from the desk, slung them over her shoulder and turned to him. "Then I'm ready."

She bestowed a sweet smile on him. It was one of her tactics for handling obstreperous people. They didn't know what to do in the face of such gentle forgiveness for their churlish ways. It was very effective.

He gave a sort of surprised snort under his breath and followed her out, turning off the lights and making sure the lock clicked into place behind them at her request. Outside, he held the door to the pickup open, took the baby while she climbed inside, then strapped the baby into her seat.

Molly tucked a light blanket around the child. It wasn't until Sam climbed in that she realized there might be a problem.

The front seat was distressingly intimate with her stuck between him and the baby's car seat. She could feel his body heat all the way down her left side. Once in a while his shoulder brushed hers as they rounded a curve.

Keeping her feet to one side so he wouldn't touch her leg when he shifted gears, she asked, "How is the cow?"

"What?" He roused out of his deep, dark thoughts long enough to glare at her, making her wonder why he'd bothered to invite her out. He certainly wasn't in the mood for company.

"The cow that had trouble calving. Is she all right?"

"Yes." He dropped back into the brooding silence.

She forebode to give him a lecture on manners. If he hadn't wanted her to come, why had he invited her?

Well, that was easy to answer. Guilt.

He'd kept her waiting four times in the past ten days. She'd let him know the last time that she expected him to be on time to pick Lass up. After all, she had a life, too.

Right. She'd been late for the monthly meeting of her literary club. Big deal.

However, the sharing of thoughts and ideas and conversation with friends was important, she reminded herself. Reading gave one entry into another mind, sometimes into a life so different from one's own a person was startled by it.

"I beg your pardon?" She realized she'd missed some mumbled message from him.

"The truck stop. Is it all right?"

The dining room at the truck stop was a popular place. Most of the people in the surrounding ranching community ate there at least once a week. It would be crowded on Friday night. Everyone would see them together.

For a briefest instant, she wondered what the local citizens would think—the local nursery schoolteacher with the local black sheep. "The truck stop is fine."

He pulled into the driveway and parked. "Wait," he said in a commanding tone and slid out.

He came around and removed the infant car seat from its straps, keeping Lass in it. The baby made noises to her father and smiled widely at him, eliciting another of those brief, but fiercely loving glances.

Molly slipped past the car seat base and jumped to the ground. To her surprise, Sam took her arm and escorted her inside. Several heads turned when they entered the dining room.

Nearly every table was full, and two of them were occupied by parents whose children came to her nursery school. She gave them a smile that said she had everything under control and this was a perfectly normal outing of the schoolmarm with the rancher and his baby. It was a good thing they couldn't see the flutters taking place inside her.

The waitress, a young woman in tight jeans, led them to a booth. Sam and Lass took one side. Molly took the other. She laid her coat beside her. He looked around for a place to put his hat. She indicated the seat beside her. He handed it over and she placed it on her coat, feeling the Stetson had been given into her guardianship just as Lass was each morning.

They studied the menus in silence, then ordered when the waitress indicated she was ready. When the girl walked away, a vacuum surrounded the table. It filled with uneasy silence. Molly waited for her companion to speak.

"I'd better feed her before she realizes she's starving," he said, indicating Lass. He reached into the side pocket of the diaper bag and fished out a spoon and a jar of cereal with fruit.

Molly watched in perfect fascination as Sam Frazier, tough, rarely smiling rancher, fed his baby with the utmost gentleness and care. When he wanted Lass to open her mouth, he opened his and said, "Ahh."

Lass imitated him.

He used the opportunity to stick another spoonful of food into her mouth. Then he smiled at the trick he'd played on her. She smiled back, nearly losing the bite. He caught it on the spoon and scooped it back into her mouth with the touch of an expert.

Molly's heart melted. "The doctor's office called today. It's time for Lass's six-month checkup."

He flicked her a glance, then nodded.

"You could come in and have lunch with us the day of the appointment," she suggested. She liked for parents to take part in their child's life as much as possible. "It would be good for Lass," she added at his unreadable glance.

"We'll see."

Not exactly a promise, but she knew he would. He'd do anything for his daughter. The baby had him wrapped right around her finger. Molly had known that the moment he brought the infant to the nursery school.

Normally she didn't take children under six months, but Lass's mother had died in childbirth. Sam had taken sole care of his tiny daughter for two months, then asked if Molly would take her during the day. She wasn't sure why she'd broken her own rule and agreed.

"Why don't you hire someone to stay at the house with Lass while you do your work?" she'd asked.

"I don't have anyone I'd trust with her," he'd answered in his blunt, but honest way. "Everyone knows you run the best nursery school around and that your reputation is spotless."

She'd preened a bit at the time. And from such moments, fantasies were born. For the first month, she'd gotten shaky whenever he came for Lass, knowing he'd never give her a glance.

Time and lack of nourishment had starved those dreams into thin, pale images barely remembered now. She wondered if he was still mourning the loss of his wife.

Their food came. He finished with Lass and gave her the rabbit to chew on while they ate.

"This is very good." Molly was determined to make pleasant conversation. A relaxed atmosphere aided the digestion.

He glanced at the cashew chicken dish she'd ordered and nodded. He continued with his steak.

A half a pound of red meat. She hoped he didn't eat that way all the time. Ranchers worked very hard and burned a lot of calories, but all that fat and cholesterol wasn't good. However, she wasn't going to expound on that. Dinner should be enjoyable.

"I wonder if the weather pattern is going to hold another week." Ranchers were always concerned about the weather so she knew it was a topic Sam would be interested in.

He gave a noncommittal grunt.

She felt her hackles begin to rise. She really hated to lose her temper. It was so uncivilized.

"Someone said the Pecos was near the top of its banks in several places south of us," she continued.

He paused and frowned. A shrug of his shoulders indicated there was nothing he could do about the river if it flooded.

Molly chewed, swallowed and patted her mouth with the napkin before she spoke. "Mr. Frazier, it is considered polite to respond when someone is talking to you." She gave him a sterling smile that, combined with the reprimand, usually brought about the desired change in behavior.

He gave her a long perusal, studying her as thoroughly as a horse buyer looking over stock that was being touted as prime and suspecting it wasn't. He had a way of gazing at a person from under those dark, imposing eyebrows that was intimidating.

She hadn't studied motivational psychology for nothing. "It is also considered correct to engage in conversation during a meal. We are not primitives, are we?"

A flash of emotion went through his eyes. She thought perhaps she'd gone too far, that he was furious. Then he smiled.

His teeth were startling white against the duskiness of his skin. His father had had some Mexican and Indian blood, she'd heard. Certainly he didn't look as Anglo as his name implied.

Except his eyes had tiny flecks of gold mixed with the brown, she noticed for the first time. Like hidden treasure.

"No, ma'am, we're not," he replied solemnly.

She stiffened, wondering if he was making fun of her. She did tend to be a little . . . stuffy. Inhibited was the term her parents had used when she frowned upon their hedonistic behavior. Prudish was the teasing way her brother had put it.

However, she decided her companion was no more prone to uncalled-for levity than she was. "Good," she said approvingly, drawing a sardonic glance from him.

"It was raining when I left the house, but I think we're getting the dying gasp of the storm," he said, picking up her conversational tidbit. "I rode the river today, checking for erosion along the banks, but everything looked fine."

"I'm sure that was a relief. We've had so many floods the past few years. The ranchers must worry each time a cloud appears on the horizon."

He laughed suddenly, unexpectedly. She stared at the tanned column of his throat. He'd bathed and shaved before coming to pick up Lass. His face was smooth, and she got a whiff of his after-shave once in a while. His jeans and white shirt were fresh. He'd rolled his sleeves up, exposing tanned forearms with fine black hairs sprinkled generously over them.

For a second, she had the oddest sensation . . . as if she'd like to kiss him, right where his neck joined his shoulder. And perhaps along those strong cords running up his throat. The impulse to do so was almost irresistible.

She cleared her throat. "Do share the humor, Mr. Frazier."

His laughter was brief, but a smile lingered at the corners of his mouth like the promise in a rainbow. "I was thinking of clouds. That seems to be all that's on my horizon these days."

"I see." She instilled the proper amount of sympathy in her tone, indicating a willingness to listen if he wished to talk.

"Please, call me Sam."

A definite change of subject. She followed his lead. "Is that short for Samuel?"

"No. It's just Sam. Sam Watson Frazier."

"Is Watson a family name?"

He shot her a glance from under the dark slash of his eyebrows that made her heart jump erratically. "It was my mother's maiden name."

"How nice. I think names are so important. They convey a sense of continuity, handed down from one family member to another like that. I'm named after my grandmothers, Millicent Dorothea."

"I thought you were called Molly."

"I am. I chose Molly when I was four and refused to answer to Millicent thereafter. My parents thought the name suited, so Molly I've been ever since."

"You must have understanding parents."

"They're very liberal, one might say."

"Might one?"

There was the slightest sarcastic edge to the question. She ignored it. "Yes, indeed. Interesting, too. In fact, most people find my parents fascinating. Actually I do, too."

He nodded, but said nothing as he concentrated on his meal once more. Sam. She mentally tried the name, picturing herself saying it to him. After months of thinking of him as Lass's father, it sounded odd, much too personal.

"Your accent is Eastern. Where are you from?" he asked after a bit.

"A tiny hamlet in Virginia."

"Did your folks object when you moved out here?" He seemed sincerely interested in her answer.

"Actually they were horrified, but then they said it was like me."

"How's that?"

"Contrary." She smiled nostalgically. "My parents said I was born to be their conscience."

His eyebrows rose fractionally. "Were you?"

"Not really." She was never less than truthful. "However, I was rather a sober child and I worried about things..."

"What things?"

"Starving children and...and things like that. I used to send my allowance to a fund for feeding the children until the counselor at school called my parents in to ask if I needed to be on the free lunch program. They were pretty angry with me over that one."

"What else did you do?"

She tried not to feel flattered at his obvious interest. After all, this wasn't a date, merely a recompense on his part for keeping her late. "I fed a starving dog once. It followed me home, so I took it to my room and let it sleep with me. It had some kind of seizure the next day. My father had to shoot it. Then I had to take rabies shots."

"Dangerous," he murmured. "What else?"

"Another time I brought home a kitten from the woods. I was so disappointed when my mother told me to take it back at once."

"Your parents wouldn't let you have pets?"

"Not this one." She looked down as if saddened by the memory. "It was the prettiest kitten, too—black with a silver line on its head that divided into two lines along its back."

When she looked up, she saw comprehension and amusement flash into his eyes, followed by a low, genuine chuckle, unlike that earlier hollow parody of a laugh. She smiled, enchanted by two surprising dimples at each side of his mouth. She hadn't noticed those before.

"I think you were a trial to your folks," he commented.

"I'm afraid so." She paused. "Were you?"

He was silent so long she didn't think he was going to answer. Instead he gazed into her eyes as if looking into her soul. It unnerved her. When the waitress stopped and poured more coffee in Sam's cup, Molly was relieved.

When they were alone again, he studied Lass, who had fallen asleep, before glancing back at Molly. "My dad died when I was twelve. I hated my stepfather."

"That's sad," she said quietly. She had very firm ideas of how families should support and love each other. "I adore my parents and my brother. They love me, too, although they find me as perplexing as I find them."

"Because you're quiet and they're flamboyant?"

His insight was startling. "Something like that," she murmured. "Um, this is quite good." She indicated her chicken dish. "How's your steak?"

"Great. I rarely get steak. My cooking tends toward the quick and easy."

"I thought all ranches had an irascible old cook who dribbled ashes into the pots and shot anyone who complained about the food."

He shook his head. "I can't afford one."

The hardness crept into his voice. She guessed his pride was pricked at having to admit he didn't have a lot of money. His life had been hard, it appeared, then to lose his wife and have a baby to take care of... Her heart went out to him.

She tried to stifle the feeling, knowing herself to be the softest of soft touches when it came to another's pain. If ever there was anyone less needy of her pity it was Sam Frazier.

During the rest of the meal, she was aware of the glances directed their way and wondered if others saw their being there as a date. The spinster and the cowboy. It was almost a parody of every dime novel ever written.

Except she was real, and so was he.

After he cleaned up every bite on his plate, he ordered more coffee and settled back in the booth with a tired but satisfied sigh. "I could go to sleep right here," he told her.

"Please don't. You're too big for me to carry."

His eyebrows jerked upward in surprise. He studied her for a long minute before asking, "Would you take me home and tuck me into bed the way you do Lass when I bring her to your nursery?"

Chills tumbled down Molly's spine at his sexy question. He probably didn't realize how provocative he'd sounded, his voice dropping into a deeper, quieter register while he spoke.

She glanced into his eyes. The dark intensity of his gaze stalled any answer she might have made. Words went flying out of her head. Then the expression disappeared, leaving her to wonder if she'd imagined it.

"You're not a baby," she finally said.

"No, I'm not." He frowned suddenly, as if realizing he'd said too much. "How did you happen to start a nursery school?"

She relaxed. The nursery was dear to her heart. She had definite ideas about the learning experiences of young children.

"Most adults have very little conception of the learning capacity of children," she said, launching into one of her favorite topics. "For instance, Lass already knows to push a blue button when she wants to hear music, a red one when she wants food and a yellow one when she wants to play with a mobile over her crib."

"Is this learning or training them like Pavlov's dogs?"

"Oh, no. Babies know what they want. Lass won't ask for food if she isn't hungry. If you offer to push the red button for her after she's eaten, she pushes your hand to one of the others, then smiles when the music plays or the mobile lowers."

"So maybe my kid's a genius?" The hard-edged question was skeptical of her conclusions.

"Lass is very bright," she informed him. He didn't seem to be taking her research seriously. However, she'd already had several articles published in various parenting magazines. "Most people don't realize how much children absorb before they're able to talk and express themselves coherently."

He nodded and looked again at his sleeping daughter. Molly realized she was lecturing him on the subject. Heat crept up the back of her neck, and she shut up.

Really, she didn't know why she always had this propensity to expound upon a topic until she bored everyone into a stupor. That had been one of her problems in high school and college, her mother had told her.

Her serious nature coupled with strictly average looks hadn't garnered her many boyfriends, although both males and females had regarded her as a friend. People had always come to her for advice. Her teachers had complimented her on being levelheaded.

Glancing at the man seated opposite her, she wished she wasn't quite so pedestrian. If she were more... exotic... maybe he wouldn't be sitting there with his head resting against the back of the booth and his eyes half-closed, studying her as if she were from another planet.

Oh, well. She finished her tea and laid the napkin aside. "I think it's time to go home. I'm tired, too."

He nodded and sat up straighter. He signaled for the check, paid it, then lifted the car seat with the sleeping Lass.

Molly spoke to several couples on the way out, people she recognized from the local church. Sam nodded but spoke to no one. She wasn't surprised.

The local people viewed him with suspicion and, as far as she could see, he made no effort to change their minds about his character.

Some folks said he'd married his wife for her money. Molly didn't believe the rumors. He was too straightforward, too bluntly honest in his dealings with her to be conniving.

Of course she did tend to take the side of the underdog...or outcast, in this case. She didn't tell him that. He wouldn't appreciate the gesture.

Chapter Two

Sam leaned against the window frame, his stance deceptively calm compared to the frustrated rage he felt inside.

"Marriage. That's my best advice," Chuck Nader said.

Sam glanced at the attorney, then back at the busy street below. "What's your second best?"

"Take the kid, leave the area, change your name and go into hiding until she's eighteen."

Sam dismissed the suggestion with an angry snort. This was his and Lass's home. They weren't leaving.

He'd been a drifter for a few years after getting out of school. He'd left the ranch that had been his heritage because of his stepfather. He wasn't about to take to the road again.

When his mother had died, the land had passed to Sam. He'd returned home and fought his stepfather for possession of the ranch that was rightfully his.

For the past two years, he'd worked hard to pay the taxes and mortgage and get the place back on its feet after his stepfather had drained all the cash he could, using the ranch's money to set himself up in an easy life-style down in Texas. Sam clenched his fists in useless anger.

This land represented his past and his future. He would guard and nurture it. Someday he would pass it on to Lass. He wanted her to grow up on Frazier land, to know her heritage and love it with the same intensity he experienced when he rode over its broad mesas and hidden arroyos.

He cursed aloud, but it didn't relieve the rage.

"Tisdale isn't going to give up easily," the lawyer said. "He needs the money. If he has custody of his grandchild—"

"And the two hundred grand that goes with her," Sam added.

"Right. With that money, he'd be sitting pretty."

"Until he ran through it the way he did with his wife's inheritance." Sam ran a hand over his face, feeling the utter frustration of trying to deal with the situation.

It looked as if he was going to be involved in another legal battle. He was in charge of Lass and her trust fund. He'd set up the blasted thing for her.

His former father-in-law fancied himself as a wheeler-dealer. Mostly he was a loser. He'd gone through all the money he could get his hands on. Now he wanted Lass's fortune.

Over Sam's dead body.

Sometimes he worried it might come to that. William Tisdale was getting desperate. Two hundred thousand dollars would go a long way toward relieving his worries. The Tisdale land was mortgaged to the hilt. Tisdale assumed the Frazier ranch was, too. It wasn't, thanks to Sam's depleted savings.

Sam cursed again. "I feel so damned trapped."

"Marriage is the best way out," Chuck reminded him. "My sister said she saw you and the nursery schoolteacher at the truck stop Friday night. The woman is perfect. I couldn't have picked a better candidate if you'd asked me."

"Molly," Sam said.

"What?"

"Her name is Molly."

The attorney hooked a leg over the arm of his executive chair and grinned. "Yeah. Molly Clelland. As I said—she's one hundred percent perfect. The minute you're married to her, Tisdale won't have a leg to stand on if he takes this to court. Her reputation is impeccable. Half the county would testify on her behalf. And yours... if you're married to her."

"I haven't touched a penny of Lass's money, not a red cent. There's no way he can say I'm a fortune hunter... or an unfit father. I don't even look at women, much less bring any home. Tisdale hasn't a chance of winning, not based on the truth."

Sam paced the narrow space between window and the chair he'd sat in briefly when he'd arrived to discuss the charges being threatened against him by his wife's father.

His father-in-law had accused him of wasting Lass's inheritance. An out-and-out lie. The old man had also implied he had evidence that Sam was an "unfit father."

Such talk had scared him. While he knew he loved Lass and would defend her from harm with every drop of blood in his body, he also knew evidence to the contrary could be fabricated against him. He remembered reading about a case in which a man had been convicted of child abuse and imprisoned for three years before it was found to be a false charge by a vengeful ex-wife.

That was one of the reasons he'd put Lass in Molly Clelland's nursery school at his attorney's urging. The respected teacher could see that Lass was a healthy, happy baby who showed no signs of abuse or neglect. He intended to see that she stayed that way. Give Lass to his lying s.o.b. of a father-in-law? No way.

"All right," he said as if facing the firing squad.

Chuck looked amazed. "You'll marry her?"

Sam set his hat on his head grimly. "I'll think about it," he said, mainly to get the attorney off his case.

"Listen, I'll have my wife invite the two of you over for dinner so you can see what married life is all about." The attorney paused to laugh. "I'll tell Janice she can't nag or scold me while you and the teacher are there."

"Sounds like real married bliss," Sam scoffed.

Chuck grinned secretively. "Oh, it is. You'll find out." He became serious. "Call me before you do anything drastic. We'll have to work out the prenuptial agreement first. Okay?"

"Sure." When he thought about marriage, Sam got a smothery feeling in his chest.

He'd thought he was in love with Elise, but it wasn't long after their marriage that he'd realized she'd married him to spite her father. Marriage to him had been her final rebellion against the old man. Within six months, she'd been restless and ready to move on...until she'd found out she was pregnant. Then she'd been as mad as hell at *him*.

When he'd reminded her it took two to produce a child and she sure as hell had been a willing partner in their marriage bed, she'd screeched like a fury. Six months later, she'd died during the birth—a stroke induced by the high blood pressure caused by the birthing process. He'd watched helplessly during the ordeal.

The doctor had explained about the weakness in the wall of the blood vessel, that the stroke could have happened at anytime and, in fact, would have happened sooner or later without the pregnancy. The explanation hadn't relieved Sam's guilt. He'd been the one who'd insisted she go ahead and have the child.

And now his father-in-law was out for his blood. And his child. Lordy, how complicated life got.

He was tired of hassles and legal wrangling. He was tired of people looking at him suspiciously as Tisdale spread lies about his marrying Elise for her money. He was tired of worrying all the time.

He had placed all of his wife's money, including the life insurance, into an irrevocable trust for Lass. However, irrevocable trusts could be broken if a person knew the right lawyers and judges. And Tisdale knew them all.

With that rustling episode from his past, Sam figured the odds were against him. If his father-in-law had his way, he would be in prison for his wife's death. As it was, the man was doing everything in his power to make life miserable.

Sam clenched a fist. Let Tisdale get his hands on sweet, innocent Lass? Never.

Marriage wasn't something he looked forward to, not even for Lass and God knows, he'd do anything for his child, short of murder. Marriage might be the only way.

"Think about it," Chuck advised, sympathy in his gaze, his manner serious once more.

That his attorney looked upon the threat from his father-in-law with misgivings scared Sam even more than the scenarios he'd already formed in his own mind. To lose Lass, the one good thing in his life... It didn't bear thinking about.

"Yeah, right." Sam headed for the door after giving his lawyer and friend a wave.

Downstairs, he sat in his truck, his brain in a whirl of half thoughts and plans. It was Wednesday. He'd called Molly and told her he was coming in for lunch today and would take Lass for her doctor's appointment afterward. She'd sounded pleased.

He tried to picture marriage to her. The image wouldn't come. She was Lass's teacher, a nice, neat, sort of preachy little woman, but not his type.

Although she did have the most marvelous eyes—gray and lucid, like a mist off the mountain.

He paused and envisioned those cool eyes gazing up at him in the heat of passion. To his surprise, his body stirred. Well, hell, he wasn't dead, after all, but... marriage?

It was the last thing he wanted to think about. Besides, why would she want a down-at-the-heels rancher and another woman's kid to take care of? Shaking his head, he turned the key and headed for the church.

Marriage? Surely there was another way.

* * *

"I couldn't believe it when my mother told me you were there with Sam Frazier," Tiffany said. She rolled her big blue eyes heavenward before focusing on her boss once more.

Molly and Tiffany were resting while the children ate their lunch. It was one of the few quiet times they had during the day and a welcome break for them.

Molly swallowed a bite of turkey sandwich, then turned to her helper. "What's so odd about it? He took me to dinner because he was late again and wanted to get back in my good graces. After all, we run the best nursery school in the state."

Her smile was composed and calm. Over the past five days, she'd reasoned away the fantasies induced by the dinner...and the strange desire to kiss his neck and snuggle her face in the black springy hairs showing above the V of his shirt collar.

"Well, of course we do," Tiffany said in a "that goes without saying" tone. "It's just that...well, watch out for him is all I can tell you. I've heard things..." Her voice trailed off in warning.

"What things?" Molly took another bite of sandwich.

"About him and his wife." Tiffany stared into the middle distance with a frown of concentration. "I went to school with Elise Tisdale."

Molly wanted to ask a hundred questions about the woman, but she refrained. It wasn't any of her business.

"She was very popular. You know how some girls have this way about them, as if they were born knowing everything? She was like that—knowing and sexy and beautiful."

She would be, Molly thought, refusing to let the information send her into the doldrums.

"In a wild sort of way." Tiffany finished her comments thoughtfully.

"Oh?"

"She skipped school a lot and was sort of, like radical, if you know what I mean."

"Actually I don't," Molly said, avid with curiosity about the woman he'd married. She imagined him looking at his wife in that sweet, fierce, loving way he showed only to his child.

"She hated anyone telling her what to do. Sometimes she'd do things—chew gum in class, smoke in the rest room—just to show the teachers she could. And she always drove like the devil was on her heels. The rest of us admired and envied her. We wanted to be like her, but few of us had her daring."

"I always obeyed the rules," Molly admitted.

"Me, too." Tiffany sighed. "I guess we were a couple of stick-in-the-muds. Or is it sticks-in-the-mud?"

"Either way you're probably right." Molly met her friend's eyes, and they both laughed. "There are worse things to be, I'm sure."

"Yeah, but nobody's thought of 'em yet. I would have given my eyeteeth to be the daring, devil-may-care person Elise was. It was such a shock when I heard she'd died. She wasn't even my friend, but it was like a light going out. I mean, she'd been so vibrant and all. I couldn't imagine anything snuffing out that spark of... of wildness she possessed."

"I understand," Molly said, remembering the girls like that in her own high school and college classes. They were self-assured, their stride confident as they whizzed through life and love, doing what they wanted, often getting by on charm.

Molly'd been smart, but then she'd always loved books and reading. She was a natural as a student, given her quiet, reserved ways. She wasn't a great beauty and wit like her mother, who'd been the most popular girl in her class.

"We all have different talents and virtues," she added for Tiffany's sake. "You're wonderful with the children."

"Because you've taught me so much. Every child we accept seems to be a genius after six months under your care. I don't know how you do it."

"It isn't me. I merely try to bring out the child's natural curiosity and channel it." She stopped and sighed. "Don't get me started. You know how I am."

Tiffany nodded and rolled her eyes again. "Do I ever!"

They were still smiling when Sam Frazier walked in the door. "I came for lunch," he announced.

Sam felt like a fool. It was obvious he was way too late for the meal. The kids had eaten and were napping now. The two teachers were finished, too.

"Looks like I'm too late," he muttered, trying to get himself out of this gracefully. "Actually I came to take Lass to the doctor."

Molly stood. "You're not too late. We're having turkey sandwiches today. Would you like one or two?"

"Uh, one." He took his hat off and stood in front of the door, not sure what to do.

"Join us," the other woman invited, indicating a seat at the desk.

"Thanks, Tiffany." He glanced toward the swing where Lass slept peacefully, then looked at Molly.

"I'll only be a minute," she told him, giving him a pleasant smile. She hurried to a little alcove at the side of the room and began preparing a lunch for him.

He hung his hat on a hook and took the regular-size chair behind the desk. The rest of the chairs in the room were scaled for the children, including the two Molly and the other teacher used. He was glad he didn't have to sit in one of those. He'd have probably broken it.

Feeling like an oversize Goldilocks, he settled into the chair and watched Molly's efficient moves. She wore calf-length gray slacks that were full like a skirt and a red sweater. She looked as chipper as a robin.

With the overhead light shining on her face, he noticed how smooth and delicate her complexion was. A man would have to be careful not to mar that skin when they made love. He looked away.

The other teacher was watching him with open curiosity. He felt the heat creep up his neck. She frowned as she glanced from Molly to him. A subtle shifting of her features indicated her suspicions of his motives.

Ha, if she only knew what his attorney had proposed, she'd probably be warning Molly away from him at that very moment!

He gave the woman a slow, deliberately bland smile that didn't tell her a thing. He didn't care what the people of the town thought of him. He'd written them off years ago when no one, including his mother, had believed his stepfather was stealing from the ranch.

No, he wasn't going to marry again. He couldn't believe he'd even considered it. He'd tried once and it had been pure hell for the most part.

However, he figured if he was seen with Molly, if people realized they were friends and she trusted him, well, that ought to be as good as marrying, but without the complications.

When Molly returned, he thanked her for the meal as she set a plate containing a turkey sandwich and various vegetable sticks before him. There were also three potato chips.

"That's all that were left," she said apologetically.

"It's plenty. Sorry to barge in on you so late."

"No problem. I'm delighted that you could join us. We usually eat around eleven-thirty since the children are hungry by then." She placed a paper cup of lemonade by his plate.

He was reminded of his elementary days at a country school near the ranch. They'd had to carry their lunches since the school didn't have a cafeteria.

Glancing at Molly, his thoughts traveled far from his own school days. He'd caught a whiff of some light cologne when she'd leaned forward to place his meal on the desk. Suddenly he wanted to nuzzle along her neck and discover exactly where she dabbed the floral scent.

Damn Chuck for his crazy ideas!

He forced his attention to the sandwich, which had cranberry sauce rather than mayonnaise spread over the bread. It moistened the turkey and added a tangy taste to the meal.

"This is good," he told Molly.

"I'm glad you like it."

Her smile was one of approval, and he experienced a surge of pride as if he'd done something especially nice in complimenting her on the food.

He noticed her teeth were very straight. Probably braces as a kid. Everything about her bespoke neatness and wholesomeness, of the mind as well as the body. She'd probably be shocked at some of his thoughts.

"Lass was very good this morning, but she'll probably be cranky this afternoon," Molly told him.

He looked at her in question.

"She'll have the last of her shots today and may run a fever as a result. Ask the doctor about giving her some baby acetaminophen when you put her to bed tonight."

"I will," he promised. He cleared his throat, then glanced at Tiffany.

She immediately rose. "I've…um, got things to do." She disappeared into a room at the back of the school.

Sam finished the lemonade and cleared his throat. "Would you like to go to a movie Friday night?"

Molly gave him a blank look and didn't answer.

He tried again. "Over in Roswell there's a movie that got good reviews. It's about a teacher in Australia. I thought you might like it."

"Well, actually I have plans. The literary club is having a potluck dinner at my house. A local writer is going to be our speaker. Would you like to attend?"

"Yes."

She seemed taken aback at his quick acceptance. He was a little shocked, too, he realized. But if they were to become friends, it was a beginning. Satisfied that his plan was in progress, he smiled.

So did she.

Her mouth trembled a bit at the corners. He noticed her lips were evenly balanced between the upper and lower one and that her mouth was a little wide. Her face reminded him of a cat with its small, pointed chin and flaring cheekbones.

He wanted to taste her, to see if her lips were as soft as they looked...

"It's at six-thirty. You don't have to bring anything. I mean, I'll have plenty. I'm going to bake a ham."

"That sounds good." He stood. "I guess I'd better get Lass on down to the doctor's office. I hate to wake her, though."

He retrieved his daughter from the swing. She opened her eyes, grinned at him, then laid her head on his shoulder and went back to sleep. He felt the familiar tug in his chest at her trust in him.

Molly held the door for him to go out. "Are you going to bring Lass back this afternoon?"

"If you don't mind. I have some errands in town. I thought I would do those this afternoon, then pick her up when I finish."

"That will be fine."

She closed the door after him. After strapping Lass into her seat, he glanced back at the nursery. Molly stood at the door, watching him with a curious expression on her face. He wondered what she was thinking. Probably questioning his motives in asking her out Friday night.

He leapt into the truck and drove off. For the first time in months, he felt something like peace inside. With Molly as his friend, he and Lass would be okay. Friday night he would start a campaign to become the very best friend she'd ever had.

Molly frowned at the empty road. Sam Frazier was late. She sighed and settled into the rocking chair.

"This little piggy went to market," she said, wiggling Lass's fingers as she quoted the nursery rhyme.

The baby gurgled with laughter when she finished with an exaggerated "wee-wee-wee all the way home."

"Ah, what a doll you are," she murmured.

Sometimes when she thought of being thirty-two and not being married, regret would set in. She felt a flutter of it now. She might never have a child, never hold a baby of her own, never have the warm companionship her parents shared so joyfully.

She hadn't thought of the future in those terms in a long time. Until recently. Until Sam and Lass Frazier had come into her life.

Recalling Tiffany's description of Sam's late wife, she smiled at her musings. While she wasn't a knockout, a couple of men had been interested in her in college, but there'd been no spark. No male had ever enticed her into the mating dance.

She wasn't the only one. Twenty-two percent of the American population never married, if she remembered the statistics correctly. Wedded bliss didn't appeal to everyone. She'd chosen her own path, and most of the time she was content.

The wind blew around the corner of the building, a mournful sound that brought the hair up on the back of her neck.

Where *was* Sam Frazier?

He arrived at ten to six, rushing in on a gust of wind, looking handsomely disheveled. He removed his hat and smoothed his hair. "Sorry. My errands took longer than I expected. I brought Chinese." He held out a white bag.

His grin was so engaging, Molly found she couldn't stay mad at him. "If that's an apology, I accept. I'm starved."

"Me, too." He spread the feast on the desk, then took Lass while Molly washed her hands and was seated.

"I fed Lass her supper at five-thirty," she told him. She spread a "busy" mat on the floor that had mirrors and rattles attached to it. "Put her on the mat. She likes to play there."

He put the baby on her stomach and watched her tug at a huge button before putting it in her mouth for a taste. Molly watched the play of emotion in his eyes before he turned to her.

She let him have the teacher's chair while she sat on a tall stool. He loaded up a paper plate with chow mein, fried rice and a chicken dish, then handed it to her.

"No sweet-and-sour pork or Mandarin beef," he said pointedly. "I remember you ate chicken last week and frowned upon my steak."

She was embarrassed at being so obvious. "I didn't realize I looked so disapproving."

"Very schoolmarmish," he told her solemnly. His eyes filled with amusement, and she realized he was teasing.

It was so startling, like standing by a statue that suddenly started speaking. "You have a sense of humor," she exclaimed.

He nodded and swallowed before speaking. "I guess I haven't been very cheerful lately. Things have been tough."

"On the ranch?"

"Well, there, too, but mostly with my father-in-law."

Molly shifted uncomfortably, recalling Tiffany's gossip about his deceased wife. She gave him a sympathetic smile.

He seemed to take that as encouragement. "He thinks he'd be better at taking care of Lass than I am."

She was shocked. "I don't. Lass is one of the happiest, healthiest babies I've ever seen."

"I'm glad to hear you say that." He ate in silence for a minute, then looked up at her from under the dark slashes of his eyebrows in that intriguing way he had. "Would you say it in court if we needed you to?"

She stared at him, wondering if there was trouble here that she didn't know about. Slowly she nodded.

"Would you?" He pressed on, his gaze intensifying.

"I wouldn't have said it if I didn't think it true."

He heaved a sigh of relief. "It won't come to court, not if I can prevent it, but my attorney suggested I line up my best shots. Just in case."

"Of course."

His eyes took on a warmth she'd never seen in them. They seemed to deepen as he stared into her eyes as if looking into the farthest recesses of her soul. She sat very still.

"Has Mr. Tisdale tried to take Lass from you?" she asked.

"He's working on it. He has a private detective following me around." Sam shook his head. "As if I wouldn't realize it. Around here, the man stands out like a crow among sparrows."

She laughed at his comparison. "Both of which are nuisance birds," she said pointedly. "Is that your opinion of people in general or the ones around here in particular?"

He smiled, and she was enchanted.

"Not all people," he murmured. "Some people are okay." He looked straight at her. "Very much okay."

Flutters raced from her throat to her stomach and back. Heavens, if she felt this way at an implied compliment, she'd probably faint if he so much as touched her... if he kissed her.

She drew back from the idea. A couple of dinners together did not constitute a raging affair. At best, maybe a tepid friendship. All right, a growing friendship, she decided, liking the way his eyes kept going to her lips when she spoke.

He wanted to kiss her. She was certain of it. Well, almost certain. He was staring at her mouth.

Which meant she probably had a grain of rice sticking to her lip. She wiped her mouth with a napkin.

"The groundhog saw his shadow, so we'll have six more weeks of winter," he told her. "Personally I'm ready for some sun and balmy skies. I've been mending fences so I can move the cattle to new pasture. It's hell working outside in a cold rain."

"You need a warmer coat. I've noticed you never wear anything heavier than that denim jacket." She pressed her lips firmly together and shut up. She didn't need to lecture him as if she were his mother.

"I wear a ski jacket and a rain slicker on the ranch. They're too bulky in the truck, so I switch to come to town."

"That's good." Oh, heavens, she sounded so stuffy. Her family was right. She was a throwback to some other era.

He spooned out another plate of food for himself after offering her seconds, which she refused.

"Tell me about your ranch," she said invitingly. "Does it have a name?"

"It's called Diablo Mesa Ranch." He studied her for a moment before he continued. "It's on the El Camino del Diablo."

"The Devil's Highway?" she mused. "What's it like?" She pictured a barren, hardscrabble place.

"It's the most beautiful place on earth." His expression softened the way it did when he looked at his daughter. "The ranch lies along the Pecos, so we have running water all year."

She altered her image to a lush, green valley.

"We're on a high, flat mesa—"

"What is a mesa?" she interrupted him to ask. "I mean, is it a mountain or what? Some people have said it is. Others told me it isn't."

"It's the flat-topped part that's left when the rest of a plateau erodes." He made a broad, sweeping gesture with one hand. "This area was once a tableland that was shoved into a tilt sloping from the northwest to the southeast when the Rockies thrust their way up through the earth's crust. Erosion has cut gullies and ravines through it. Mesas form where a harder layer, such as cap rock, protects that section of the plateau from the weathering effects of rain and wind."

"Ah," she murmured in understanding.

"The ranch house sits on a rise above the mesa. From it, you can see eternity—" He halted abruptly, as if he'd said too much.

He had shared part of himself with her, she realized. He knew and understood the land as keenly as any geologist. More than that, he had a vision within himself of the land, with him a part of it. This place was home to him as it was to her.

"Do you have gullies and ravines?" she asked softly.

"Yes. They're mostly dry washes—arroyos, the Spanish settlers called them. I've dammed some of them on my land to form ponds, but they go dry a couple of times a year, so it isn't a dependable source of water."

"I see."

At her interest, he expounded on the land and what he'd like to do someday "when I strike oil or a gold mine."

She smiled at his wry crack.

"You have a nice smile," he said, startling her.

"Thank you."

"You should smile more."

"So should you," she responded in her usual tart way. She clamped down on the inside of her lip. A lecture wasn't the way to a man's heart.

A stillness came over her while she contemplated the question that leapt into her mind. Was she aiming for his heart?

No, of course not. It was just a thought.

Chapter Three

Molly pushed the cat out of the way with her foot and checked off the items on her mental list—ham, rolls from a local bakery, freshly made cookies. All was ready for the potluck dinner honoring the local author.

"You've had your dinner," Molly reminded Persnickety, who pressed against her leg and made cat sounds of starvation. "Be nice like your sister. She's not begging for a bite of ham."

Porsche snoozed on the throw rug by the back door.

Molly heard a vehicle in the driveway. She glanced at the ham on the table, then at the black cat with three white whiskers. "I don't trust you," she declared. She ushered both cats out the back, then rushed to the front door.

"Am I too early?" Sam called, climbing out of his truck.

He looked very presentable in dark wool slacks, his usual white shirt—open at the collar, the sleeves rolled up. He carried a bouquet as he came up the flagstone walk.

"No, of course not. Lass will be glad to see you." She'd brought the child home with her after the nursery school closed.

He handed over the gift at the door, then took off his hat as he stepped inside. She watched his gaze take in the small house with its spit-polish shine.

She'd worked all last evening to make sure it was perfect. As if she'd wanted to impress him. For a second, while they stood there, suspended between one moment and the next, she tried to analyze her feelings. She shook her head hopelessly.

"Lass is in the kitchen," she told him, leading the way.

She was aware of him following close behind. His after-shave drifted on the air, mingling with the tiny dabs of perfume she'd put behind her ears.

All her senses seemed heightened. She felt the silky swish of her dress against her stockings. Her friends from high school and college had all told her she had nice legs... really nice legs. The blue silk dress, a gift from her mother, cleared her knees by an inch or more.

Spinster tries to seduce cowboy, she mocked. As if that would be possible. She hadn't a sexy bone in her body.

Sam hung his hat on an old-fashioned highboy and followed her into the kitchen. "Smells good in here," he murmured.

Soaking up the flavor of the place—the aroma of home-cooked food, the lemony scent that bespoke cleanliness and a tantalizing whiff of mingled cologne, soap and powder that shouted *woman* to his starved senses, he realized how bare his own life had grown.

For a second, he imagined this was his home, all clean and shining, his dinner, hot on the stove, his wife and child, eager to welcome him with smiles and kisses.

He took a step forward . . . A babble of sound from Lass kept him from making a fool of himself. He changed his direction and headed for the playpen.

"Hello, sweetheart," he said, scooping Lass up and tossing her toward the sky.

She squealed in delight. "Da, Da, Da, Da," she said.

"Da-da," he encouraged. "That's me, your old man. I'm the boss and don't you forget it, young lady."

Lass pulled his nose.

"Hey," he scolded and dodged the moist tug.

He glanced across the tiny kitchen. Molly was watching them, a gleam of approval in her eyes. A smile glazed her lips.

Her mouth looked soft and inviting. A rosy pink shine indicated lipstick. He realized she'd rarely worn any on the days when he dropped Lass off at school. Odd, he'd never missed it on her.

His wife had used a lot of makeup and had looked pale without it. She hadn't liked for him to "muss" her up. The sure knowledge came to him that Molly didn't have those vanities. His glance strayed down her slender curves.

Molly was aware of his perusal with every nerve ending in her body. She busied herself with the flowers.

She knew he was looking at the sheer black stockings she'd worn with three-inch evening pumps. Somewhat irritated by her own vanity, she wondered if women teetered around on high heels to indicate they'd like to be swept off their feet.

That was obviously the last thought on her guest's mind. He hugged his child to his chest with a protective arm under her bottom and a hand on her back and continued talking to her.

"Hi, how's my girl?" he questioned in a soft voice.

Lass clicked her tongue at him. He laughed and clicked back at her. When he glanced up and saw Molly watching, he looked sort of sheepish.

"I took her riding with me a couple of weeks ago," he said. "She heard me click my tongue to the mare and has been doing it ever since then."

"Yes, babies are great mimics."

"Guess I'd better tell the spring roundup crew to watch their language from now on."

"I thought roundups were in the fall when ranchers sold their cattle."

"I hire on a couple of extra men to help with the branding and all. They usually stay until after the cattle are sold."

"I see. Then you're alone the rest of the year?" She thought of him on the ranch, alone during one of the blizzards they occasionally had.

"Yes."

"I'm sure it's beautiful, but isn't it lonely?"

"No."

Her eyes met his at the quick, harsh denial. Their gazes locked and wouldn't let go as they engaged in some primal clash that shifted her equilibrium. A knotty sensation settled in her throat as she wondered wildly what he was thinking.

Lass's head, with its soft wisps of cottony curls, bobbed against Sam's chin, severing the unexpected tension that had leapt to life between them.

Full of nervous energy, Molly busied herself filling a vase half-full of water, adding two tablets as a preservative and poking the bouquet of daisies into it. She placed the flowers on the table behind the platter of ham.

The bright yellow blossoms looked nice against the earthy red of the tablecloth.

"Still life with ham," she said, standing back so Sam could admire the effect. She glanced at him. The moment of awareness between them when she'd mentioned the loneliness of the ranch might never have been.

She drew a calming breath. "I think I hear the others arriving. Shall we go into the living room?" She glanced back over her shoulder. "Lass has had her supper, so she should be okay until bedtime. Do you give her a bottle then?"

"Uh, yes." He looked up.

His attention had been on her legs. A light fluttering invaded her middle. She was intensely aware of her short skirt, the silky dress...the heat that tumbled out of some place inside her as if the door to a furnace had been opened.

Most of the literary club arrived together. "Come in," she invited the preacher and his wife.

Mrs. Liscomb checked on the threshold, causing her husband to stumble over her. The knot of people behind them halted.

"Do all of you know Sam Frazier?" Molly asked, standing back so her guests could get a clear view of him standing behind her.

Aubry Liscomb's jaw actually dropped open. "Sam Frazier," she echoed.

Sam watched surprise segue into animosity from several of the locals, the ones who'd lived in the community when he'd left and had still been there when he returned. Old resentment welled up in him, hot and churning. The residents had always been a bunch of sanctimonious hypocrites as far as he was concerned. They hadn't changed a damn bit—

Molly took his hand, forcing him to step forward and acknowledge her guests. He sliced her a glance and saw the expectation in her eyes.

He sighed internally. The prissy little teacher expected her guests to be on their best behavior... including him. He clasped her hand tightly when she would have removed it. He'd be nice if it killed him, but he deserved a reward for the effort. Touching her was it.

"Evening, Mrs. Liscomb, Reverend," he said.

"Evening, Sam," the preacher said. He gave his wife a gentle push from behind. She mumbled a greeting and stepped into the room. Sidled was more like it, as if she'd be attacked if she got too close.

Sam forced a smile on his face. He wanted Molly for a friend. That meant he'd have to accept these people, too. He let go of her hand reluctantly so she could perform her duties as hostess. When the guest of honor arrived, he moved back to her side, standing close so that she was aware of him. He smiled at her startled glance, then spoke to the man whose book had won some prize or other; he remembered reading about it in the paper. He laid his hand at the back of her waist.

Molly felt warm the rest of the evening and didn't catch more than one word in three of the guest speaker's lecture on the terrible state of American art and government funding for it. Sam's eyes were often on her, a quiet watchfulness in the rich dark depths.

A quietness grew in her, too, as if she were waiting…

Lass slept peacefully in the playpen in the study off Molly's living room. Sam stood watching her from the doorway, his thoughts on other matters.

He couldn't believe the evening had gone so quickly. He'd actually enjoyed some of it. Except when that windbag writer had held Molly's hand for a long time at the door while he told her what a delightful time he'd had. The man was interested in Molly. That much was clear.

Sam frowned in irritation. His carefully constructed plans didn't allow for outside interference.

Another problem was Molly herself.

She'd thrown him for a loop when she'd opened the door and invited him inside. Gone was the school-teacher who handed out advice on child rearing or one's manners. In her place…God, in her place was a stunning woman.

He closed his eyes. Soft. That was the impression she gave—a delicate softness that made a man want to reach out and stroke that smooth skin, those flyaway wisps of hair.

Yeah, but he knew only too well how fast a woman could change from a sweet, ethereal creature—loving and clinging and making a man want her so bad he'd forsake the world—and turn into a shouting fury that made him want to crawl into a hole and not come out till hell froze over.

"Well, that was the last of them." Molly's voice cut into his musing. "It went well, didn't it?"

"Yes."

She bent over the makeshift crib. "Ah, the sleep of the innocent. Lass is such a good baby, not a peep out of her about sleeping in a strange place."

Her soft voice whispered over him like a caress. Her light brown hair fell over her shoulders in a silky cloud. Her skirt hiked up to expose an enticing bit of black-clad thigh as she gazed down at the sleeping child.

He looked away and stared out the window until his blood settled down again. It had been over a year since he'd made love with a woman. His marriage had gone from wild passion to cold fury in a few short months. Abstinence had to be what had sparked this crazy desire he had for his daughter's teacher.

That and his attorney's urging him to marry her. Molly, the intelligent little prude, would probably be shocked at the thoughts that had run through his mind all evening.

She straightened and turned to him. "Would you like to leave her for the night? I have enough diapers. There's an extra outfit in the diaper bag and I can run over to the nursery for more food."

"No, I'd rather take her home."

He doubted he would sleep a wink if Lass wasn't snug in her own bed. He had a need to know she was nearby, safe and sound. The problems with his former father-in-law had made him paranoid where his daughter was concerned.

"But thanks for offering," he added belatedly, realizing how harsh he'd sounded.

She smiled graciously. "Here, wrap her in the blanket. You can return it Monday when you bring her in."

He nodded in thanks, the sense of well-being he'd experienced at odd moments all evening returning. He liked Molly Clelland, he realized.

She was a bossy woman, like most teachers, and yet she wasn't. She gave choices and coupled them with instructions in such a way that a person automatically did what she said. He found her presence soothing... for the most part, except when his libido kicked up.

They walked down the hall. He retrieved his hat and jammed it onto his head. At the door, he paused. "Listen, my attorney wanted to know if we'd like to have dinner with him and his wife sometime. How about tomorrow night?"

"I'm busy then," she said and looked regretful.

He wondered if she was saying that to make it seem as if she had lots of dates. His wife had done that. Molly's next words assured him she wasn't playing a game with him.

"Perhaps next weekend? I have both Friday and Saturday free." Her eyes held no hint of subterfuge.

"Right," he said, relieved that she hadn't turned him down. "I'll check on the day and time and get back to you."

"Fine." She stood by the door and held it open for him.

He shifted Lass from one shoulder to the other. A moment dragged by. A question appeared in her eyes.

"I had a nice time tonight," he finally said. "Thanks for having me." He stepped out into the night.

"It was a pleasure," she called after him. He heard the smile in her voice, then she closed the door against the chilly night air, and he was left out in the cold.

In the truck, after fastening Lass in her seat, he drove off quickly, feeling like an utter fool. For a moment there, he'd considered kissing Molly good-night.

She would have probably fainted or slapped him. No, she would have given him a lecture on propriety or manners or some such fool thing.

He smiled, a soft feeling stealing over him. Lass stirred and clicked her tongue in her sleep and settled again. The smile evaporated, and his thoughts returned to practicalities.

He wanted Molly for his friend, not his lover, he reminded himself. Once the sex wore off, men and women didn't remain friends—at least not in his experience. He needed her friendship.

The idea gave him pause. He didn't think he'd ever been friends with a woman before. It was a different concept.

Sure, he'd been friendly with girls while growing up and with some women he'd known. But being friendly and being friends seemed two different things.

A friend, he repeated. For some reason, it made him feel good deep inside.

Molly stifled a yawn. "Janice and Chuck are nice," she said. She and Sam had met the other couple in Roswell where they'd gone to dinner and a movie. "Have you known him long?"

She rested her head on the back of the seat and observed Sam's face from the glow of the pickup's dashlights. A terrible clenching in the vicinity of her heart worried her. She felt it each time she saw Sam, which was to say, every day.

"Only for a couple of years."

"Since you've been back home?"

"Yes. He was new in the area and an outsider." Sam cast her a glance before concentrating on the road once more.

"Like me."

"Like me," he corrected. "He's from back east. He married a local girl and settled here about the same time I returned."

"You were born here," she said pointedly.

"But I was gone for twelve years. Before that, I had a reputation for wildness."

"Did you deserve it?"

"Maybe. I drove fast. I acted tough. And I didn't like taking orders."

"Especially from your stepfather."

She saw his hands tighten on the steering wheel, then relax. "Yeah, especially from him. He waltzed into our lives six months after my father died and took over. Thought he was J. R. Ewing."

"You resented his taking your father's place. That's natural. Obviously he didn't win your trust or friendship."

"He was eight years younger than my mother and looking for the main chance. I hear he's courting a rich oil widow in her sixties down in Texas. Should I warn her he has a way of moving money from a joint account to one in his name only?" His tone was hard and cynical.

Molly made a sympathetic sound. She knew more about his past now, thanks to Tiffany and the pastor's wife. They had both warned her about becoming involved with Sam.

The preacher's wife had taught Sam in high school. "A smart boy, sailed through school making *A*'s and *B*'s without cracking a book. But he had an attitude.

Very independent. Hated taking orders from anyone. Caused trouble at home.''

Molly knew it was gossip, but she'd listened anyway.

''He hated his stepfather, who was a charming man by all accounts. However, I didn't know him. They weren't churchgoing people, you know. The ranch belonged to Sam, but his mother had the use of it for her lifetime. That might have caused trouble. Gives a young person too much sense of his own self to come into an inheritance too early.''

''Sam isn't like that,'' Molly had said.

''There wasn't much money, I understand. The Tisdale girl had money from her grandmother. He married her within a few months of moving back to these parts.''

''Because he loved her,'' Molly said softly, knowing it was true. ''He married her for love.''

The preacher's wife sniffed in disdain. ''All the men wanted her. She was like a cat, a wild one, racing around in a little red car like she owned the road. She and the Frazier boy were two of a kind. Some say he didn't want the baby and tried to make her get rid of it.''

Molly was shocked and furious, but she didn't show it. She assumed an innocent expression. ''But we know Sam better than that, don't we? Isn't it amazing how gossip gets started and spreads without any base whatsoever?'' she asked.

Mrs. Liscomb had had the grace to blush.

As well she should, Molly thought indignantly. No wonder it was so easy to plant suspicion about a person when people who should know better perpetuated the stories.

"Something bothering you?" he asked. "You huffed as if you'd just thought of something that made you mad," he added when she looked at him in surprise.

Molly relaxed. During the time she'd been seeing Sam, she'd often been amazed by his perceptiveness. "I was thinking about how gossip gets started and how it lingers."

"People been telling you to stay away from me?"

She straightened. "Sometimes you scare me. You seem to read my mind."

"You're very open and honest in your relationships and emotions. Sometimes that scares *me*."

Laughter bubbled out of her at the thought of this man being scared of anything, much less her.

"I like it when you laugh," he murmured. "It makes me think that all is right with the world."

Her world was very much all right. She'd been happy these past four weeks. She loved her work, a handsome man was interested in her, what more could she want?

"The world can be a nice place."

"Maybe."

"If we don't let our troubles overwhelm us."

"A little pep talk, teacher?"

She smiled. A deep contentment pervaded her. The inside of the truck was comfortable and cozy. The evening had been pleasant. More than pleasant.

When they'd left the movie and stood talking to the attorney and his wife beside their car, Sam had laid his arm casually across her shoulders. She'd linked her hand in his while they finished their conversation and said good-night.

The warmth of his body alongside hers lingered in her memory, causing tingles along her throat and down her chest.

They were growing close, she thought. Sam was more relaxed in her presence. During the four weeks since that first dinner, they'd gone to the truck stop twice more, then to the café in town once for lunch.

Sam hadn't been able to go to the literary meeting this month because of Lass, but he'd brought dinner to the nursery school this past Wednesday. He'd waited at her desk while the other parents picked up their children.

When she'd locked up, they'd gone to her cottage, fed Lass and eaten the roasted chicken dinners he'd brought. He'd left immediately afterward. He hadn't once tried to kiss her. Not ever. Although she'd thought he was thinking strongly about it a couple of times.

It was very confusing.

Sometimes he seemed to be . . . interested, but at others, it was as if his mind were far away, in another world.

They arrived back at her house shortly before midnight. Tiffany let them in. "Lass is asleep."

"Was she any trouble?" Sam asked.

"Not a bit. She's a doll." She patted back a yawn. "Did you have a good time?"

"Yes, it was a wonderful evening," Molly replied.

Tiffany gave her an assessing look, then flicked her gaze over to Sam. Molly could sense the reservations her friend had about her seeing the rancher outside of school hours, but she said nothing.

Molly would not tolerate any insults to Sam. He had been a perfect gentleman each time they'd been out. Of course, until tonight, Lass had always been with them.

"Good." Tiffany grabbed her coat and purse. "Well, I'll be on my way. Good night."

"I'll walk you out." Sam saw her to her car and on her way.

Molly hung her coat in the hall closet. When Sam returned, she smoothed her sweater down over her slacks, feeling like a teenager whose mother might walk in any minute and find a young man in the house.

"I'll put on some coffee while you check on Lass," she said. "If you'd like."

He nodded and strolled into her bedroom where the playpen was located. Molly hurried to the kitchen. Her hands trembled ever so little while she measured out coffee and water.

Tension gathered in her like a coiled whip. She'd felt it in the air while at dinner. Sam had watched her during the evening with an intensity she hadn't seen since the first time they'd gone to dinner.

She had noticed Chuck Nader, Sam's attorney as well as his friend, giving him a couple of sardonic glances that seemed filled with hidden meaning. Sam had frowned at the man and sent him a warning look.

Footsteps behind her sent a nervous tingle along her throat again. She spun around.

Sam stood a few feet from her. His eyes were almost black in the dim light of the lamp over the table.

She sensed strength in him, and the emotions that he kept clamped inside. She wished she had the key to free them, to let him love again the way he'd once loved.

There was no way she could give him back a happy past, to make his boyhood days the carefree, happy ones he should have had, but his future . . .

A tremor rushed through her when she realized what she was thinking. "The coffee is about ready." She sounded breathless.

He reached out and touched a strand of her hair. "Did you have a good time tonight like you said?"

"Of course."

"Of course," he repeated. "You always tell the truth, don't you?"

She was intensely aware of his hand close to her face, of the way he smoothed the curling strand over and over between his finger and thumb as if judging its quality for some purpose of his own.

"I try."

A ghost of a smile touched his lips and was gone. He released her hair and sighed. "Let's have that coffee, then I have to get home. The day starts early on a ranch."

She poured them each a cup and went to the table. Sam sat opposite her and blew across the hot surface before taking a drink. "You make good coffee."

"Thank you."

"But then, you do everything well."

"Thanks again. I think." She wasn't sure that was a compliment or not. "Do you get tired of tending the ranch? There seems to be so many problems, so many things you can't control, such as the weather, farm prices and all."

"There are times during the winter when I think an inside job would be a good idea." He grinned, then continued in a softer tone. "But when the sage is sweet and the air is balmy, when the sun shines and all the world seems right, then I wouldn't trade it for anything."

She pictured him astride a horse on a high mesa . . . king of the mountain . . . and envied him.

It was a curious emotion, envy. She realized it was the sense of oneness he shared with the land that she wanted.

Maybe dating this handsome rancher wasn't the best thing for her. He made her think of things she shouldn't. For example, she wasn't a sensuous person, yet she often thought of touching him. Worse, she couldn't seem to control the longing to do so. It was disconcerting to say the least.

She didn't think Sam was looking for a romantic attachment. However, the world must be a lonely place after having someone to share it with. A soul could wither and die from the loneliness.

A meow at the door diverted her thoughts. She reached out and turned the kitchen doorknob, letting Porsche, long, black and sleek, into the house. The cat went at once to her food bowl.

"If there's reincarnation, I hope to come back as a cat in your house," Sam told her. "Food, shelter and nary a worry."

"How long would you be satisfied as a pet?" she teased.

"Forever, if I were a cat. Not long as a man. I wouldn't fancy being kept on a leash."

"Perish the thought." She cupped her chin in her hand and leaned her elbow on the table. "I can't see you as a pet."

A flash of emotion appeared and disappeared in his eyes. "No, neither could I."

Chills chased along Molly's arm. He seemed to be speaking of something in his past. She wondered if she dared question him on it, but decided against it. He would tell her what he wanted her to know and nothing more. She'd learned that in the past four weeks.

Porsche finished her meal and leapt into Molly's lap, her purr turned up full blast. Molly stroked the smooth black fur. "Where's your playmate?" she asked the cat.

"There's two of them?" Sam asked.

"Yes. Someone dropped them near here last summer. They were mere babies. I fed them by hand for a few days until they learned to eat on their own. They're shy and tend to stay out of sight when someone is in the house." She looked up with a smile. "They've gotten used to you and Lass."

Sam watched her rub the cat and thought of that pale, slender hand stroking through his hair. His body went on red alert, and heat pooled low in his abdomen. He'd tried not to think of Molly that way this past month. It had been hard.

His adult relationships with women had been based mainly on physical attraction and the need of the moment. Since meeting Molly he'd learned the value of friendship with the opposite sex.

Her viewpoint, her opinions, her understanding of life were different from his. It had been a new experience to explore her sharp, agile mind. Glancing at the clock on the wall, he saw the hour was well past midnight.

He finished the coffee, reluctant to leave this warm, peaceful place. Maybe Molly would invite him as well as Lass to stay the night... He cursed at his wayward libido and stood.

Molly, startled, stood, too. The cat jumped to the floor, meowed with annoyance and walked out of the kitchen with a stately gait.

"I'd better go," he said.

She nodded. Her expression was as innocent as Lass's. Molly, for all her degrees in learning, never seemed to realize the times when he was gritting his teeth to control his reactions to her warmth, her scent, her womanly nature.

Tonight she wore dark slacks and a red sweater that hugged her delicate shape like the black nylons had defined her legs at the literary meeting. He wondered how he could ever have thought she was plain.

She wasn't an attention-getter the way his wife had been, but she had a muted vibrancy about her that reminded him of wildflowers in a spring meadow.

"Molly," he said. He heard the deeper register of his voice, the shift into the husky tones of desire. Since he'd stood close to her, his arm over her shoulders while they said good-night to the other couple, he'd wanted to touch her.

Really touch her.

She looked up at him, her eyes shining like a mist backlighted by the sun. The sure knowledge came to him that he was going to kiss her.

For a second his breath hung in his throat. He didn't trust his control with her, and he didn't want to frighten her. Molly was a lady; all his experience had been with a different kind of woman.

He took hold of her shoulders. His hands looked big and rough on her slender form. Her candid gaze, slightly questioning but trusting, affected him in ways he couldn't explain.

Instantly he knew without a doubt the opinionated little schoolmarm had never had a man. She had no idea what he wanted from her, of the mindless lust that could drive a person into equally mindless acts...like marriage.

It almost unnerved him.

He hesitated to pull her close, afraid that he wasn't reading her right. With Elise, it had been no problem. They'd met at a bar in Roswell. One look, one dance and they'd left the place. Elise had been all over him the minute they'd arrived at the ranch. They'd married two months later.

But this was a different time, a different woman. Molly wasn't ruled by her senses or a childish greed for pleasure and fun all the time. He watched in fascination as her tongue stole out and moistened her lips. She was nervous.

A quick kiss, just a taste, that was all he'd take, he assured himself, nothing to alarm the most circumspect of maiden schoolmarms.

He slid his arms around her, carefully, slowly drawing her close. He lowered his head, his gaze on those soft lips that now showed a tendency to tremble. The tenderness he often felt toward Lass washed over him.

To his surprise, he felt her arms lift and come around his shoulders, felt her warmth plaster itself down the length of his body, felt the richness of her generous nature as she accepted his touch.

Heat burst outward in a shower of red sparks behind his closed eyelids. Heaven. This was pure heaven. He didn't want to stop.

Chapter Four

Molly couldn't believe this was happening, that Sam was really going to kiss her, that she was going to let him.

Her eyes widened as he bent toward her and his arms gathered her closer and closer. For a second, during that endless time it took for him to span the distance to her lips, she remembered the kisses she'd experienced in the past.

Her brother had foisted dates on her a few times, buddies who came home from college with him. She generally liked people, and things usually went well until the evening ended.

Those awkward endings. The problem of where the nose went and should she breathe or not. The general sloppiness of kissing, of someone else's moisture on her lips, of sweaty hands raking at her clothing.

She'd found the whole process distasteful and had refused any further help with her love life. She grimaced at the memory.

At her frown, Sam paused. She tensed, afraid all of a sudden that he wasn't going to kiss her, but knowing she wanted him to. She just didn't know why.

After that hesitation, his lips settled on hers as lightly as a butterfly on a thistle. He closed his eyes, and she was left staring at the dark lashes that outlined his eyes. She closed her eyes, too.

She found kissing didn't have to be awkward at all. His kiss was incredibly tender, his lips barely touching hers. He moved from one corner of her mouth to the other. It was so unbearably sweet.

To her surprise, she found herself on tiptoe, wanting to do something more. She wasn't sure what. Those funny tingles that started in her throat and worked their way down her chest whenever she thought of him in a certain way, now slid hotly past her breasts and stomach until they lodged deep in her abdomen.

Her skin became hot, too. And her bones. She melted right into him, needing his arms to keep her standing upright.

Was this the passion of song and poem?

She heard his slight grunt of surprise, then his arms tightened even more. His tongue swept over her lips in a circle, making them tingle in the most delicious way. Her breath moved in and out of her lungs.

Breathing. She realized she was breathing and it felt quite normal. Except she was also quite dizzy.

Lifting her arms, she clung to his broad shoulders. The movement shifted her breasts against him. They beaded up hard and . . . yes, they tingled, too, like her lips, but different.

So many sensations assaulted her at once—the wonderful strength in his body as he wrapped his arms around her and held her closer than she'd ever been held before, the heady scent of his after-shave mingling with her own perfume that intensified as she became heated, the tantalizing knowledge that there was more to be learned.

"Open your mouth," he murmured against her mouth.

She'd seen couples in movies do that. It had embarrassed her, all that ravenous mouthing, as if they were trying to take a bite out of the other person. She crimped her lips together.

He continued to stroke her lips with his tongue, very, very lightly. It tickled. She felt a grin coming on.

He lifted his head and gazed at her from only an inch away. His stare was fathoms deep, but amusement lurked at the corners of his mouth. She felt silly. Really, this was ridiculous.

Finally she couldn't stand it any longer. Her lips softened and parted into a smile. He took advantage. His lips swooped on hers, startling her.

With sure aim, his tongue delved into her mouth.

The effect was shocking. The tingly sensation dipped all the way down into her body. A shiver attacked her as if she had a chill. At the same time, she'd never felt so hot in her life. And her heart was racing, banging away like an engine gone berserk.

His hands stroked down her back, cupped her bottom and lifted her into the cradle of his thighs as he spread his legs. A new awareness attacked her. Of him and the changes in his masculine body. Very, very masculine.

He released her mouth just in time.

"I think I'm going to faint," she managed to whisper.

"No, you're not." He kissed her eyes, her temples, her ears, then down her throat. "It just feels that way."

"For you, too?" She was amazed.

He smiled. "Not quite, teach, but close."

He shifted her slightly, setting the tingles to surging again. She thought the sensations were too strong to be called so simple a name. She just didn't know any other. Then he was kissing her mouth again, and she could no longer keep up with all the things happening to her.

She moaned and cupped his face in her hands, taking the kiss to unbearable depths of pleasure as she answered every thrust of his tongue with hers. She knew this wasn't the ultimate pleasure and wanted more. She squirmed against him.

"Easy," he said. He moved slightly, brushing against her again and again in that throbbing place she had known existed in a clinical way and now discovered in all the carnal joy of the human body.

His hands moved over her back, then one caressed along her side. They weren't sweaty or grabby at all. His every movement gave her pleasure and increased her awareness of delight. It seemed so strange to find this... like a secret garden that had existed right under her nose.

But only this man had opened the gate and invited her inside. That was the key, she realized vaguely. He coaxed and and teased and playfully guided her along pleasure's path.

It was incredibly wonderful.

Sam fought his own needs. He knew himself to be a physical person. He enjoyed using his body, whether for ranch work or other, more intimate labors. Right now, her needs were more important than satisfying an appetite of his.

He knew he could take her to bed. She was filled with the hunger of their kisses. Every caress of his had been designed to bring her maximum tactile pleasure. He wanted desperately to give her the total fireworks— the explosion of passion that would leave her sated and wondrous as she shared her first experience with a man. It was an odd feeling, one he couldn't recall ever having before. And he couldn't do it. It wouldn't be fair.

Knowing he wouldn't, couldn't take this all the way didn't stop him from wanting to, or from taking a little more of her before he was forced to stop.

He caressed the lean line of her torso, moving up and up. . . a bit more . . . ah, the perfection of it.

Her breast fit his hand. It was fuller than he'd expected, but then she didn't wear her clothing so snug that every curve was visible. With this woman, there were surprises. He wanted to discover all of them.

Only half-conscious of what he was doing, he skimmed down the red sweater, under it and back up to that perfect mound.

When she gasped, he drew back a little. She opened her eyes and stared at him, dazed, limpid and aflame with the passion he'd given her. He waited, wondering if she'd tell him to back off. It was even odds she'd never let a man touch her this way.

She didn't speak, but stood there as if waiting for him to guide her. Passion was new to her, and she didn't know what he expected. She didn't even know exactly what she wanted.

He did.

With a groan, he shoved the soft knit of the sweater out of the way and dipped his head to her breast. Through the satiny material of her bra, he found the hard peak and rubbed it with his lips, then took the succulent tip into his mouth.

He felt the passion claim her once more. She locked her arms around his neck and ran her fingers through his hair. Her breath came quickly as he sucked her.

With one hand, he unfastened the back clasp and the material slid upward. He pushed it out of the way and his mouth met flesh—warm, sweet, woman flesh. He nibbled hungrily at the delicate pink tip.

When she arched against him, they nearly lost their balance. He turned and braced against the wall, using its support to keep them upright for he, too, was as far gone in passion as he'd ever been without being in bed. Opening his legs to a wider stance, he urged her to step inside.

He laved attention on each breast until he was nearly crazy with the need to explore more of her. Her skin was delicate, and he could see the tracings of veins that disappeared under the dark pink aureole that surrounded the rosy nipple.

She would be soft and delicate in other places, too. He wanted to go lower, to stroke her into bliss while he held her and kissed her mouth and her breasts.

"Kiss me back," he said on a groan, returning to her lips.

She did what he said, raising her face to his in mindless obedience to the attraction. He was more than surprised by the passion between them. He was almost overpowered by it.

A white-hot surge of need hit him. He realized she had pressed herself solidly against him and was instinctively rubbing that part of him that wanted to bury itself in the hot welcoming center of her.

It would be sweet. It would be like heaven . . .

A screech from hell brought him back to earth.

"What the devil?" Sam said.

Molly clutched his shirtfront in fright. Then she realized what the scream was. "The cat. Something's hurt it."

She started for the door, then stopped and looked down in shock. Her bra and sweater were scrunched up almost to her neck. A tide of hot pink flowed over her face and neck. She had nearly gone outside half-unclothed!

"Stay here." Sam was out the door in a flash, leaving her to fumble with her bra clasp, which suddenly wouldn't close . . . oh, there, she had it.

She jerked her sweater down, then headed out the door as fast as her trembling legs would take her, her mind a welter of confusion. "Do you see her? Is she hurt? Is it a coyote?"

"No," Sam called. "Stay inside while I look around."

"I'll get a flashlight." She ran inside and searched through a drawer, throwing half a ball of twine, a pack of mailing labels, a box of matches and two clothespins on the floor before she found it.

She ran back out into the cold night air. The first day of spring had occurred that week, but the weather hadn't caught on yet. It was still cold and rainy. She flicked the light around the backyard and saw Sam.

A black streak materialized beside her and disappeared into the kitchen through the open door.

"There she is. She's inside. I think she's okay."

"Give me the light. I'll look around a bit more."

Molly glanced at the dark shadows of bushes and trees. The wind had risen in the last hour or so. The shadows danced eerily. Sam removed the light from her hand and headed back toward the gardening shed. She stood in the doorway and watched as he knelt and looked around.

When he finally returned, she asked what he'd been looking at or for.

"Whatever I might find" was his terse reply.

She studied his tense stance and frowning face. "You suspect something. Do you think someone was out there?"

He shrugged. "Probably a fox or a coyote," he said without answering her question.

She peered anxiously out the window, but couldn't see any signs of anything wrong.

"I have to go." He locked the back door and made sure it was secure. "I should have left an hour ago, then we wouldn't have gotten into...what we did."

"Are you sorry?" she blurted. She realized she wasn't.

"I..." He rubbed a hand over his face. "I'd like to remain friends with you. You're the only one I have." His smile was filled with irony.

"That's not true. What about Chuck Nader and his wife? Others around here would open up if you'd make the first move." She crossed her arms over her chest and gave him a stern look. "You might try smiling and saying hello to people."

"Yeah, I might." He looked down at his shirt, looked grim for a second, then began tucking it into his pants.

She must have pulled it loose. She could remember running her hands over his back, liking the feel of his firm flesh and the flex of muscles she could feel under the skin.

Heat rose to her face again. She'd never known she had the capacity to be a wanton. But perhaps every woman had. With the right man.

"I'm going." He hesitated. "Is it okay if Lass stays?"

"Yes." She nodded several times as if the answer wasn't enough to convince him.

"Lock up after me." He headed for the front door.

She followed and turned the dead bolt securely after him. He paused at the truck, raised a hand in goodbye and left a minute later. She watched until he was out of sight.

Sam attached the wire to the connector and made sure it was secure, then leaned on the corner post and looked at the sky. Not a cloud to be seen. Well, a few horsetails floating above the Pecos, but nothing to worry about.

Spring had painted the pastures in shades of vibrant green. The grama grass sprouted lush new growth. Actually the rains had arrived at just the right time that year.

Calves cavorted beside their placid cud-chewing mamas in several sections. It was time to move them to new ground. He twanged the electric wire once more to be sure it was firm, then went to connect the battery.

This was something new he was trying—moving the cattle across the pasture in blocks of heavy grazing, then "resting" the grass until it recovered. An electric fence provided a simple and cheap method to keep the cattle in the right section.

Down at the county road, he saw the postman stop at the mailbox. He decided to ride down and pick up the bills. He smiled a bit grimly. His mail rarely contained anything else.

Swinging up on a big-boned roan gelding that had a gait like a rocking horse, he headed down the ranch road, one eye on the stock fence as he went. A sense of accomplishment brought a lightness to his heart that had been missing for years.

The ranch's affairs and his personal affairs were in good order. He'd paid off all debts to his attorney and the bank and had enough money to make it through the year. If the Good Lord was willing and the creeks didn't rise... And if the rains kept coming so the pastures would grow. And if no one started a prairie fire. And... Well, the list could be endless, but today, he didn't care.

His friendship with Molly was paying off. The owner of the local general store had actually smiled at him when he walked in the other day.

He grinned at that and whistled the rest of the trip. At the end of the road, the gelding sidled close to the mailbox so that Sam could lean down and collect the mail and the newspaper.

Feeling the friskiness in his mount, Sam chuckled as they wheeled around for the return trip. "Yeah," he agreed, "I've got a touch of spring fever, too."

He patted the horse's neck in sympathy. "Poor chum, you don't even know what it's all about, do you? You just feel the urge without knowing how to take care of it."

With a subtle shift of his body, he gave the gelding tacit permission to run. The big horse took off toward the barn and the oats he knew would be there for him.

Sandy, one of the two men he'd recently hired, waited by the stable door for them. "Somethin' after you?" he asked when Sam swung down and handed the reins over.

Sam laughed. "Only kicking up our heels a bit. Must be spring fever."

The young man grinned in understanding. "Come Saturday night, I'm heading for town. Come on, you bag o' coyote bait," he muttered to the horse. "Stop prancing around like a derby winner. You ain't worth . . ."

Sam flicked through the mail while he crossed the unmowed patch of grass that constituted the lawn around the ranch house.

Nothing but bills, he noted as he leapt onto the porch without making use of the two steps hewn from giant cottonwoods and went into the kitchen. One letter was from the bank.

He opened it, expecting an advertisement for an investment opportunity the bank advised him not to miss. Instead he found one of his checks had been returned for insufficient funds.

Cursing under his breath, he called his attorney from the wall phone in the kitchen. "The bank says my check to you was returned. I don't know why. I made a deposit last week from the spring sell-off."

"I knew it was okay. Call the bank," Chuck advised. "They probably credited it to someone else. Let me know when to send it through again. By the way, are congratulations in order?"

Sam was instantly on guard. "What for?"

"You and the schoolmarm. I've heard from three different sources that things are pretty hot between you two. One of them was my wife, so the women are speculating about you, too."

Sam cursed aloud. "What exactly have you heard?"

"Well, you had your arm around her outside the movie the other night. Lots of folks saw that. Then there's talk that you didn't go to your house after you took her home that night." The attorney's voice took on a cautionary tone. "Don't forget those prenuptials. You need an agreement before you take the final plunge. You don't want to put the ranch in jeopardy in case the marriage doesn't work out."

Sam gripped the phone, recalling scenes from Saturday night. Him with Molly locked in his arms. Kissing. Touching. His hands on her breasts. Her hands under his shirt, her eyes closed, her teeth clamped on her bottom lip as he kissed and sucked at her bare nipples. The wonder and confusion in her eyes when they'd finally come up for air.

Some friend he was. Because of him, people were talking about her, questioning her virtue. Because of his inability to control his baser impulses, she was the center of gossip.

After hanging up, he called the bank.

"That was an out-of-town check," the woman in accounting explained. "It takes three business days to clear."

With any of the other local ranchers, the bank would have held the check until the deposit cleared, but no one trusted him. Except Chuck. And Molly.

From the bank teller's disapproving tone, Sam was sure the older woman had heard the gossip, too.

And he knew exactly where those rumors had started. He'd found footprints out by Molly's shed. The detective he'd forgotten about in the blaze of passion had lost no time in letting Tisdale know.

"Is the money in my account now?" he asked, reining in the sarcastic remarks on the tip of his tongue. Molly would have told him such tactics only alienated people. Not that he gave a damn. At least, not for himself. But for her...

"Yes," came the snooty reply.

"Thanks." He hung up the phone none too gently, anger getting the better of him.

Grabbing the truck keys, he went outside and took off in a shower of dust and gravel. In fifteen minutes flat, he stomped the brakes in front of a two-story Tudor-style mansion and came to a screeching, skidding stop.

He leapt to the ground, slamming the door behind him so hard the truck trembled on its shock absorbers. Elsie Tisdale opened the door before he had time to knock.

"He isn't here," she lied, wringing her hands together at her waist. She was a short, skinny woman who reminded Sam of a plucked chicken. "William isn't home."

"Excuse me, ma'am." Sam stepped by her and walked into the study, done up in the manner of an English gentleman's club, to the right of the hallway.

William Tisdale, his former father-in-law, glanced at him, then screwed his face up as if he smelled something rotten. "What the hell are you doing here?"

"I came to see you about a small matter." Sam rocked back on his heels. "Such as the rumor floating around town about me spending the night with Molly Clelland.''

Triumph flashed through the older man's eyes before he tried to assume an expression of righteous distaste. "Your prurient activities don't interest me in the least.''

Sam strained to keep his temper under control. Tisdale was a bastard, he'd known that for two years, but he couldn't afford to let the man get the best of him. Lass depended on him.

He carefully unfolded his hands from fists and tucked his thumbs into his back pockets and assumed a relaxed stance. He smiled, and for the first time alarm flashed through the gray eyes across the desk.

Briefly he wondered how gray eyes that looked like mist in sunlight when they were Molly's eyes only reminded him of vermin when they belonged to his former father-in-law.

"Maybe this will interest you," Sam said softly. "A check in the amount of two thousand dollars paid to a certain fleabag detective from a, shall we say? somewhat shady law firm who also happened to receive a check for a like amount the same day from a certain rancher from hereabouts.''

"Oh, William, what have you done?" Elsie Tisdale had come into the room unnoticed by the two males. She hovered by the desk, her thin legs trembling like a tired roadrunner's.

Tisdale's face turned an interesting shade of purple. His eyes shifted from his wife to Sam, then away from both of them. "You can't prove anything," he blustered.

"I can prove invasion of privacy. That's a felony." Sam felt no triumph in winning a battle against his former father-in-law. He wanted peace and quiet and the opportunity to raise his child without fearing for her future. That's all he wanted.

Elsie gasped and made little sounds as if she were a chicken with a piece of corn stuck in its craw.

Tisdale stood and leaned over the desk. "Get out of my house. You're not welcome here. You never were. You never will be. And don't think that goody-goody teacher can help you. She's as much a part of this as you are. If that dolt of a detective had had a camera, I could prove it."

Sam straightened from his don't-give-a-damn slouch. "Leave Molly out of this. If I hear one more word about her..."

He let the thought trail off, realizing he'd left himself open when a gleam appeared in the older man's eyes. Tisdale now knew Sam had a vulnerable spot besides Lass.

"You'll what? Sue me?" The older man thought he had the upper hand. His smile was full of malice. "You bring that baby here where she belongs and Saturday night will be forgotten."

"Lass," Sam said tersely. "Her name is Lass. Or Elizabeth Gail if you prefer to be more formal."

"How is she?" Elsie asked.

She wore such a pathetically eager expression that Sam felt sorry for her. The woman hadn't seen her granddaughter since Sam had taken Lass home from the hospital. He hadn't thought to invite the woman over to the ranch.

"You can come see her." He gave William a warning glance, then spoke again to the timid woman. "But come alone. You can visit with Lass, but no one else."

William leaned across the desk with a roar. "She's not going to visit anywhere. You seduced my daughter and sweet-talked her into marrying you, but you're not going to ruin my granddaughter's life the way you ruined my girl's. If she'd come home to us, she'd be alive today."

Tisdale knew how to kick a man where it hurt the most. Sam flinched inwardly, but showed no emotion.

"She left this house because you made her life miserable," he said, interrupting the tirade. "Whatever else was between us, she trusted me. She left me in charge of her inheritance, not you. And every penny of it is in an irrevocable trust for Lass."

"An irrevocable trust!" Tisdale exclaimed. His face turned pale. He slumped into the richly padded leather of the executive chair. "I don't believe you."

"It's true. And in case you get any ideas about my dying soon, my attorney and the bank are the alternate trustees. I've made provisions for Lass's care as well."

Tisdale assumed an aggrieved air. "The child needs her own family. No court in the world would give her to someone who isn't blood kin, and I know you don't have living relatives."

"But they would give her to her mother."

"Her mother," Elsie echoed. She swayed as if a wind whipped around her frail body, as if she might snap right into pieces. "Elise...Elise is dead. Lass has no mother."

Sam took the woman's arm and led her to a chair. She collapsed into it, uncontrollable tremors running over her.

"Yes," he said gently, "Elise is gone."

"Thanks to you," William snarled behind him.

Sam faced the man and his unreasoning hatred and greed. "But I'm not. I'm alive. I can marry again and give Lass the family you say she needs. My wife would be her mother." He smiled at this winning thrust.

"Wife?" Tisdale taunted. "What decent woman is going to take a man everyone knows married his first wife for her money, then forced her to have the child that killed her?"

Sam took a deep breath. "My fiancée," he replied calmly. "Molly Clelland."

Chapter Five

Molly clapped her hands and led the singing while Tiffany banged away on the old upright piano in the corner. The twenty preschoolers marched around in a snaky circle, some with drums and triangles, which they clanged with great enthusiasm while the rest sang.

It wasn't until the door opened and Sam entered that she realized he was on the place. Tiffany had opened the nursery that morning while Molly ran errands. She hadn't seen Sam when he'd brought Lass.

Heat rushed into her face and neck. She hoped she wasn't as bright red as she felt.

The morning after. Although this was a couple of days later, she understood that expression perfectly now and wondered if she would be less or more embarrassed if they had consummated that torrid session in her kitchen.

Smiling with a calmness she was far from feeling, she left the children and crossed to Sam's side.

"Hello," she said above the din. She bravely met his eyes, then as quickly looked away. She didn't know how to handle the fact that this man had seen more of her than any living person. Except her doctor, who was also female, and of course her mother had taken care of her when she was little.

But no one knew her body the way he did.

Saturday night, with her blood hot—another expression she could now fully appreciate—and her mind in a whirl, her wanton conduct had seemed natural and right. But in the cold light of day...

Oh, heavens, those clichés... they were all too true.

"I need to talk to you," Sam said, leaning near her ear so he wouldn't have to shout. "It's important."

Misgivings churned like a whirlpool in Molly's stomach. Something was terribly wrong. She'd never seen him look so grim. Or angry. She nodded.

Looking across the room, she caught Tiffany's eye and motioned that she was going to step outside. Tiffany nodded and, not missing a beat, took over the singing, adding her voice to the children's boisterous trebles.

In the crib, Lass slept through the racket without a twitch. Molly saw Sam's eyes on his daughter. She recognized the fierce vulnerability he tried to hide.

Grabbing her jacket, she led the way outside. Sam followed and walked with her along the path. She headed for the creek, which had calmed into a gurgling, fast-running brook.

He stood by her without speaking for a couple of minutes. Instead he looked into the clear water as if seeking answers to questions he couldn't speak aloud. She waited.

Finally, he turned to her. "Saturday night," he began. He took off his hat and ran his hand through his hair. "Something's come up..."

Her gaze flew to the snug-fitting jeans and the point where his zipper started.

His snort of laughter was harsh. "Besides that."

A wild blush erupted. This time she didn't have to wonder. She knew she was as red as the proverbial beet. Her knowledge of the male anatomy wasn't as clinical as it had once been, and her dreams of late had been shocking. She folded her arms across her waist and waited for the bad news.

"Molly." His eyes searched hers.

She saw supplication in those lucid depths, but she didn't know what he wanted from her.

"Ah, God, Molly, I'm sorry," he murmured and surprised her by taking her into his arms.

She didn't know if he was trying to comfort her or be comforted, but whatever, it was obvious something was troubling him.

"Sam, what is it?" She put her arms around his waist. He'd been working and hadn't stopped to change clothes. His scent reminded her of sunshine and hay fields and of... um, yes, of horses. She breathed deeply.

"How can I help?" she asked, leaning her head back to gaze into his troubled expression.

"Would you consider marrying me?"

She waited for the words to make sense. It had sounded as if he'd asked her to marry him. "I beg your pardon?"

His grin was brittle. "Yeah, I know. I've probably shocked your logical little brain, but after Saturday night . . . we have to get married." He finished the sentence in a rush.

She still couldn't figure this out. "My brain is full-size, I'll have you know," she informed him, convinced he was making a joke and she was the brunt of it. She hadn't thought he was a cruel man, but now she wondered.

Sam touched her forehead, then lifted a strand of hair that blew to and fro in the mild March breeze. The air was crisp but balmy, the sky was clear, the sun was shining. All should have been right with the world.

When Molly peered into his eyes, her own lucid gray ones confused and somewhat wary, he experienced a desire to gather her close and protect her from all the hateful things in the world. She would be mortified if she heard the rumors flying around the county about them.

At the gas station, when he'd stopped to fill the truck, he'd nearly gotten in a fight with a ranch hand from the spread east of his place. Sam had gone to school with the man. The cowboy said he hadn't realized the nursery schoolteacher was such a sexy dish until Sam started taking her out.

"Let me know when you get tired of her," the lout had said.

Sam had informed him in deadly tones that Molly was his fiancée. By now, that statement was all over town. He had to let her know before she heard it from someone else.

He didn't give a damn what anyone thought of him, but he couldn't let her be hurt. He hated Tisdale for forcing them into this position. He hated the gossip-

mongers of the town. Most of all, he hated himself for
having put Molly into it.

Molly, the sweet and innocent. Molly, the virgin.

She hadn't really known how to kiss. That had
nearly blown his mind. But she caught on quickly. By
the time they came up for air, she was giving as well as
taking.

He could still remember the feel of her hands running over his back, the sweet scent of her clean, delicate body, the sight of her translucent skin with the
veins tracing faint blue paths on her breasts. He broke
out in a sweat.

Dammit, he was marrying her for her sake, not his.
He'd not let sex come between them again. Not until
she was sure she wanted the marriage.

Marriage. The smothery feeling settled in his chest.
His first marriage had been a disaster, once the passion wore off. But this was the only way he knew to
protect Molly. The honor of his name, such as it was,
was all he had to offer her.

"I hate to rush you, but I have to have an answer,"
he said, prodding her when she remained silent.

"Now?"

The word came out a startled croak. He had to smile.
For once, the mouthy little schoolmarm was without
the proper advice and reprimands, it seemed.

He nodded. Pushing his hat off his forehead, he took
her by the shoulders and faced her squarely. "After the
other night, we both know it's inevitable."

He looked away, unable to face the clear honesty of
her gaze. He didn't want to see the hurt in those eyes
when she heard the rumors. He had to protect her.

A hollow feeling hit him in the gut. Marriage. The
thought of it weighed on his chest. He'd never had a

friend like Molly before. He wondered if they could continue the same way after marriage as before—as friends.

Maybe without the confusing issue of sex between them, they could. He'd give her that choice.

She took a deep breath and forced herself to meet his gaze. "Yes, I know. It was..."

"Yeah," he agreed, feeling like the lowest snake in the world. He was using her, her friendship, the passion that had grown so unexpectedly between them. He had to tell the truth. "However, there's another problem. Lass's grandfather is giving me a hard time." Well, that was part of the truth.

Molly nodded. Others, as well as Sam, had told her of the troubles between him and his former father-in-law.

"With us married, it'll solve several problems. I need someone I can trust to take care of Lass. In case something happens to me," he added.

Her mouth puckered into its disapproving mode. She frowned at him. "I don't want to hear that kind of talk. Nothing is going to happen to you."

"Not if I can help it," he agreed with a grim smile. "But I have to be prepared. I have to know Lass is in good hands."

"I understand." She stepped into his arms and hugged him fiercely, proud that he'd come to her. He hadn't said the words, but none were really necessary. She knew his heart. And her own. "Of course I'll marry you."

His embrace tightened into a bone-crunching hug. He lifted her from the ground and swung her around.

"Help," she cried, laughing with the joy that invaded her like a shining light. "You're squeezing me to death."

He put her down at once and lightened his hold. "You won't be sorry," he murmured huskily, pressing his face into her hair. "I swear. You won't be sorry."

"I know."

She snuggled against his shoulder, then with a daring she'd never had, she kissed along the base of his throat and up the cords of his neck.

He laughed, and for the first time since he'd arrived and called her outside, she sensed the easing of anger in him.

"We'll get a license right away. Today."

"We have to get blood tests first."

His gaze was tender. "Ever the practical one. Okay, let's go do it."

"Wait!" she pleaded when he started off for his truck, towing her along like a startled heifer.

He stopped. "Make it fast."

She folded her arms and gave him the teacher's stare, which didn't daunt his good humor at all. He winked at her and waited.

"First of all, a marriage is a partnership," she began when she recovered from the charming grin he bestowed on her. "I intend to be a full partner, so don't think you can boss me around."

"I am the boss. And I'm bigger than you." He folded his arms across his chest, mimicking her and obviously enjoying himself now that he had her agreement to his mad plan.

A delicious shiver splashed down her spine. Marriage. She hadn't dared let herself dream of anything coming from their friendship. And now *this*.

Of course she'd known how she felt, that she was falling in love and trying very hard not to. But now she didn't have to hide her feelings anymore.

Oh, love was wonderful! It was just like the songs said.

"Second, I'm not going to have a hurry-scurry wedding like some kid in trouble." Her neck grew warm, but she persevered. "The people at church will expect a decent wedding. My parents will fly out. My brother." She totted the numbers up on her fingers as she counted. "And I want an engagement ring."

"My mother's is in the strongbox at the ranch. I thought you might like it . . . you know, continuity and all that stuff."

She was pleased and touched that he remembered her little sermon about that and family names. "I'll be a good mother to Lass," she promised. "I already love her."

He heaved a deep sigh. "I know. That's what makes this so much easier."

Easier? A strange word.

"That and the fact that you're such a good sport about it all. I'll be a good husband to you," he said. He hesitated as if unsure of his next words, then added, "I won't rush you or anything. I promise. I know marriage will be new to you. We'll take things slow and see how they work out."

She hadn't the foggiest notion what he was talking about. A thought came to her. "Sam, how old are you?"

"Thirty-two."

"When was your birthday?"

"A couple of months ago. My doctor can give you a written report on my health if you're worried—"

"No, no. It's just…I'm thirty-two, and I wasn't sure if you were a couple of years younger." She peeked at him through her lashes. "I'm almost six months older than you are."

"That much?" He looked amazed. "You're remarkably well preserved for an old lady." Then he laughed before she could get more than moderately indignant. "We'll have a proper wedding, but let's hurry. It's important to me that we get things settled as soon as possible. I'll feel a lot better about Lass and the ranch when we're married."

"Oh, Sam." She hesitated, then flung herself into his arms, teary-eyed at his trust in her.

"Let's go get the blood tests. The nurse said she could take care of it whenever we stopped by."

"You've already asked?" Molly thought of people all over the county speculating about Sam's plans.

"Yeah. Can you leave now?"

"Let me help Tiffany serve lunch. We can go during nap time." She held his hand as they walked back up the hill.

Marriage. She couldn't believe it. She, who had made up her mind long ago that she was destined to spend her life alone and had actually been content with the idea, was marrying the most exciting man in the county!

"Shall I tell Tiffany?" she asked before they entered the nursery. She felt shy all of a sudden.

"The more the merrier," he told her.

A slight cloud appeared on her horizon of happiness at the grim determination in her fiancé's eyes.

"Is there something more you're worried about?" she asked.

Sam looked into Molly's beautiful gray eyes and saw her soul. Honest, trusting, candid. Molly thought everyone was as kind and decent as she was. She appeared happy about their marriage. He wondered if she thought she was in love with him.

He shied from the thought. Love was just another name for lust, an insanity that made a man make mistakes. He and Molly were friends. Friendship was good. It would form the basis of a solid marriage. He would have to control his wayward instincts and forget the way she went wild in his arms.

"Have another," Mrs. Liscomb urged.

Molly declined another cookie. "That was delicious."

The preacher's wife fluffed the ruffles over her ample bosom. She served ornate teas at the parsonage on Sunday afternoons. Molly had been invited for the last serving. No one else was there. She braced herself.

"It was certainly a surprise about your engagement," Mrs. Liscomb told her.

She gazed at the ring on her finger. The diamond flashed brilliantly in the light from the window. Everyone in town wondered if she knew what she was doing. All the old rumors regarding Sam and his first marriage had been dusted off and brought to her attention.

"To me, too," she admitted. "I mean, I knew how I felt, but I wasn't sure about Sam." Her tone said she was now and nothing could change her mind.

"One doesn't want to be hasty."

"No, one doesn't," Molly agreed. "Sam and I are both over thirty, so we're old enough to know what we want. It wasn't a snap decision." After all, they'd been dating for a month before he'd kissed her.

And what kisses they had been. She could hardly wait to try some more of them. When he had sucked and stroked her breasts, it had stirred the wildest sensations. She wished he would do that again.

Heat rushed through her, and she was embarrassed at her own wayward thoughts. She would never think of her body in quite the same way as she had before that tender assault.

Her most womanly assets were places of joy and pleasure, she'd learned, not mere physical representations that she was a female. She was still amazed at the potential for response that lived in her. She'd had no idea—

"You've led a sheltered life." Mrs. Liscomb was determined to carry through no matter how difficult the subject. "Sometimes a person can be overwhelmed by a man." Two red spots erupted in her plump cheeks.

Molly sighed quietly and nodded. She was going to get a lecture whether she wanted one or not.

Mrs. Liscomb mentioned hormones and the temptations of a handsome face and the perils of physical attraction. She gave a summary of male behavior. She brought in fear of being alone and growing old. She concluded that someday Molly would meet a man who'd be exactly right for her.

"I've never been afraid of being alone," Molly said. "My life has been very pleasant. I'm sure it's going to be more so. Lass is a wonderful child, and Sam is a wonderful man."

Mrs. Liscomb glared at her as if she were being particularly dim-witted about the whole thing. Molly smiled serenely.

She knew she was doing the right thing. Sam needed her. Together they'd make a home for Lass.

Flutters dived from her throat down into her chest. She wondered if she'd have any other children. A brother or sister for Lass would be nice.

She stood. "Thank you for tea. I'd better be going. It will be time for the evening service before you know it."

The minister's wife accompanied her to the door, put out by her guest's refusal to take her sage advice, her concern giving way to irritation in the face of Molly's stubborn complacency.

Molly walked out the door and across the road to her own snug cottage with a happy step.

She quickly changed clothes and jumped into her car to go to Sam's house. He'd invited her out for a cookout and to look the place over so she could plan what changes she wanted to make. Sam had told her to do whatever she wanted about the furniture.

The drive took forty minutes. She thought of him driving back and forth twice a day to leave Lass at the school, then pick her up. A devoted father.

He and Lass waited on the broad Spanish-tiled patio. She parked and went up the path, noticing he'd used Southwest plantings in the garden. An unmowed patch of bunch grass formed the lawn.

"This is delightful," she told him after they'd exchanged greetings. They were almost formal with each other.

"I don't have time to mow," he explained about the grass.

"It doesn't need it. This looks lovely and natural, like a small meadow. The dry creek is a lovely touch."

She was aware of his eyes on her. In jeans and a loose shirt, with her hair in a clip at the back of her head, she probably looked more like a teenage baby-sitter than the woman he would marry the second Saturday in April. Only a bit more than two weeks away.

"Did you talk to your folks?" he asked.

A flush seeped into her face. "Yes. They'll be here in time for the wedding."

She didn't tell him that after a stunned silence, her mother had declared the news "wonderful!" and followed by asking if she were "in the family way?"

"Sam is a gentleman," she'd reprimanded her erring parent.

"Yes, but you're getting married so soon. I always thought you'd insist on a year's engagement at the very least," her mother had teased, "just to be sure you were suited."

Right now, Molly was wondering if she and Sam were suited. He was often distant around her, his mind preoccupied with other things. He'd made no move to kiss her again.

She'd observed him for over six months. Sometimes she thought she wasn't any closer to knowing the real man than she'd been the first time they'd met.

"Good," he said in answer to her news.

She'd insisted on waiting until her parents could join them for the occasion. Sam had no one. He'd suggested going to a judge's chambers. Her friends from church wouldn't hear of it.

"Molly must have a big wedding," Tiffany had informed him. "Everyone will want to come."

Molly remembered the way he'd gazed at her, a smile at the corners of his mouth and a look in his eyes . . . it had been almost as tender as the way he looked at his child. It had given her goose bumps.

She wished he could express what he felt in words.

Or kisses.

Heavens, she was getting so bold, she worried about herself!

"I've got the grill going. It's around this way." He led her along the porch that wrapped from the front to the back of the house.

She admired the peachy-beige stucco that glowed in the setting sun. Sam told her he had recently painted it.

While the charcoal turned gray with ash, he told her about the ranch. His great-great-grandfather had settled on the land over a hundred years ago. He'd been a land agent for the federal government, sent out to check on some conflicting claims.

She told him of her past. "My ancestors were whalers. They settled first in Boston, then on Long Island. Later, they moved to Virginia." She took Lass while Sam spread the coals. They went inside.

The kitchen was modern. His mother had had it remodeled shortly before her death. The cabinets were light oak. The counters and walls under the cabinets were tiled with white ceramic squares. Some tiles had paintings of desert wildflowers on them and were interspersed among the others.

"Oh, I love this," she said, turning all around.

"Do you?"

"It's lovely. All that counter space. My kitchen is so tiny." She stopped, coloring when she remembered what had happened in her kitchen.

"Molly, about that night," he began slowly.

Her lungs constricted at the seriousness of his tone. "Yes?" she managed to say.

"Do you have any regrets?"

She shook her head. Lass grabbed a flyaway curl and tugged. She removed the lock. "None. Do you?"

"Only that it forced a decision you might not have been ready to make. Some people will wonder about us and our marriage." His smile was cynical. "There's already talk that I seduced you into marrying me. People think I need money."

"You had a check bounce." Molly had to smile at the startled, then exasperated expression on his face. "Tiffany has a cousin who works at the bank. Do you need money?"

"No. Well, yes, but I have enough to get by."

He put Lass in a playpen and gave Molly a quick tour of the house. "You keep a very neat house," she complimented him. She glanced around the master suite. "I've never been in a man's bedroom before. It makes me feel odd."

"Odd?"

"Like I might get scolded for meddling any minute." She turned to him with a smile. "Doesn't that sound like a nervous spinster?" Her smile wilted under his keen appraisal.

"Why haven't you married?"

She'd been asked that question before. She usually replied that Brad Pitt, or whatever movie star was currently popular, had never asked her. They walked down the hallway.

"I never really had any desire to," she said truthfully. "I thought about it some when all my friends were anxious about boys calling for dates, but it never really interested me. I'm afraid I much preferred books over boys."

"Yes, you would." He nodded toward the baby from the kitchen doorway. "She's ready for dinner."

Molly noticed that Lass was sucking noisily on her fingers, a sign that she was hungry. She watched while Sam got out jars of food, warmed them in the microwave, stirred them and tested the temperature before bringing the meat and pasta combination to the table. He opened a can of pureed pears.

Molly strapped Lass into the high chair. "I'll feed her."

"Molly, about our marriage . . ."

"Yes?" She glanced at him after feeding Lass the first bite. He looked so worried.

"I care about you, about our friendship," he said, then he hurried outside to put their steaks on the grill.

Molly sighed in confusion. Something was troubling Sam. Maybe he'd tell her later. She fed Lass, then gave her a quick wash. Going to Lass's bedroom, she put a clean diaper, then pajamas on the sleepy baby.

After winding up a music box and turning out the light, she left the room and went to find Sam. It was time they had a talk.

She found him on the back porch, tending the steaks. He also had vegetable shish kebabs sizzling over the coals.

"Mmm, that makes my mouth water," she commented. She sat on the porch railing and watched for a few minutes. "What's bothering you?" she finally asked, turning her attention from the sunset to the silent man.

He placed the meat and vegetables on a platter and placed it on the warming shelf beside the four dinner rolls. "I've heard talk in town," he began. "About us."

She nodded. "I've heard the rumors. People think you've charmed me." She believed in getting things out in the open. "That you need money and that's why you want me. I've also been told the same rumors about your first marriage."

"I would never marry for money. My stepfather did that to my mother. She thought he was wonderful. Fortunately she never knew he was skimming money from the ranch and putting it in his own account. I had enough savings to pay off the ranch mortgage, so it's in the clear. I don't have a lot of cash, but I don't owe anyone, either."

"I didn't believe the rumors, Sam."

A tinge of color seeped into his face. "There's one more thing. I have some papers. My attorney thinks we should sign them. Just in case."

"Just in case of what?"

"In case the marriage doesn't work. If you want out—"

Sam stopped speaking and watched the transformation. The girlish look disappeared as Molly assumed her teacher's stance—arms crossed, feet firmly planted, eyes like spear points.

"It hardly bodes well for our future if you're already thinking of the ending before the marriage starts," she lectured sternly. "A marriage isn't an on-again, off-again thing. It's something that people work at."

"I rushed you—"

"No, you didn't. I made up my own mind."

"You've never said what you expect from marriage."

"My wants are simple. Respect and common courtesy will do for a start. I've seen people treat family members worse than they treat strangers on the street. I disapprove of that. No one deserves kindness more than the people you live with. They're the ones who will stand by you.''

Molly realized she was sermonizing and shut up. A vague alarm hummed through her mind. She felt threatened by outside forces she didn't understand.

Sam, like the preacher's wife, was determined to have his say. ''I want you to be happy.'' He gave an odd half smile. ''You're the only friend I've ever had.''

''I'm very pleased with our plans,'' she said solemnly. ''Now, where're the prenuptial agreements? I suppose he wants us to list all our assets so I won't claim any part of the ranch if we wind up divorced.''

She grinned as Sam turned a becoming shade of red and mumbled about lawyers and their distrust and all that. He hadn't learned to trust many people, but he would learn to trust her.

Laughing, she leaned close and nibbled his ear, startling him. ''I'm not your only friend, but I intend to be your very best friend for life,'' she whispered, happy that they understood each other.

Chapter Six

"You've certainly found your soul mate." Molly's mother observed Sam across the crowded reception room at the church. "He's as quiet and serious as you."

"Not all the time. You should see him playing with Lass. He's wonderful with her."

"And with you?" Her mother gave her a shrewd appraisal.

"Oh, yes," she said, so earnest and heartfelt that she blushed at being so obviously and foolishly in love with her husband.

"My darling changeling, I'm so glad for you." Her mother hugged her tightly. "I want you to have the happiness I've had with your father. Establishing a home and being true to one's vows is important. Children need constancy, but few people realize it today.

They think their own temporary happiness takes precedence over the good of their family. It's so sad.''

Since Molly was the one who usually delivered mini lectures on family life and children's needs, she was pleased when her mother expressed the same views.

"Feeling sentimental, old gal?" Mr. Clelland inquired, dropping an arm across his wife's and daughter's shoulders and giving them both a hug. "Actually, she's felt rather a failure. Here we presented the perfect marriage for our children to follow and we thought neither of you were ever going to marry."

Molly kissed her father's cheek, catching a whiff of his after-shave, a scent as familiar and comforting to her as a child's favorite blanket. "And now you not only get a son-in-law, but a granddaughter to boot."

"That Lass," her father said in loving approval.

The baby had already stolen their hearts. She had taken to them as they'd taken to her. It had been endearing to watch them *ooh* and *ah* over the child. Lass had accepted the admiration as her due and given back smiles and tongue clicks and her own mode of conversation.

At that moment, Sam looked at Molly. Her heart lurched. He was so incredibly handsome in his suit and tie, his hair freshly trimmed, his face smoothly shaved. She couldn't tear her gaze from his as he made his way across the room.

Her father released her when Sam came up and put his hand on the small of her back. "Lass is getting fussy," he said. "Shall we go?"

She nodded, unable to speak past the emotion blocking her throat. Her mother gave her one more hug. "Be happy."

"Yes, I will," Molly said, looking at Sam.

The two men shook hands. Her brother, Gareth, joined them. "Be good to her," he said as he shook hands with Sam. An implicit threat underlined the words. She frowned at him.

He hooked a hand behind her neck and gave her a kiss on the cheek. "Be happy, little sister."

Tears swam into her eyes. She and Gareth, who had been two years ahead of her, had been close during their high school and college years. He'd once been in love, but his fiancée had died in a car wreck, the victim of a drunk driver one rainy evening on her way to meet him. His grief had been deep and silent.

"You, too." She tried to think of someone she knew who might suit a high-powered attorney who argued cases before the Supreme Court. No one came to mind.

A whimper alerted her to Lass's distress. She kissed her brother and leaned into Sam. "Let's go home."

A light flared in his eyes and was gone. He let her mother kiss his cheek, then, his hand on Molly's back, he guided them to where Tiffany bounced Lass on her knee. When Molly appeared, Lass held her arms out to her. Molly hefted her new daughter into her arms. Lass settled sleepily on her shoulder.

"She'll drool on your dress," Sam cautioned. He slipped a folded diaper under Lass's head. "Let's go."

Amid wishes of a happy future, muted in respect for the sleeping child, the newlyweds made their way out to Molly's compact car. Sam strapped Lass into the car seat.

They were ready to leave. He sighed in relief.

Birdseed rained on them from the laughing crowd as he ushered Molly into the front seat. Everyone for miles around had come to wish the beloved nursery schoolteacher, who also taught Sunday school, he'd learned, good luck in her marriage.

His smile became somewhat sardonic. Molly's friends thought she would need all the luck she could get. He'd seen the concern on their faces during the hectic days before the ceremony.

He fastened his seat belt, checked to make sure his two girls were okay, then drove up the winding lane to the road and out toward the ranch. Other drivers blew their horns upon seeing the ribbons attached to the car and the writing on the windows.

On the way home, he thought of the difference between this second wedding and his first. He and Elise had had no friends to see them off. They'd been married by a justice of the peace in Roswell with no one but the old woman's husband and a friend who happened to be visiting as witnesses. It had been a spur-of-the-moment thing, performed the day after the final quarrel between Elise and her father. They'd both worn jeans.

Glancing at Molly's white dress, he struggled with a sudden ache. He wished he could offer her the same nervous eagerness he'd felt as a first-time bridegroom. He wished he could offer her his heart, pure and unsullied by reality. For some reason, he felt she deserved it.

Molly, the good, the kindhearted.

He made another vow. If, after a reasonable time of marriage to him, if she decided she wanted it to be real, he would be the best husband a woman could want. He'd cherish her. He'd be gentle. He'd never take his frustration or anger out on her. He'd remember the little things women were supposed to like, flowers and little surprises and all. He'd . . .

There wasn't a snowball's chance that he could be that saintly. He sighed. He'd do his best not to hurt her, by deed or word.

Molly's heart lurched again when Sam turned onto the ranch road. She'd been having a lot of trouble with that organ during the past few days. Whenever she thought of Sam, it would leap around like a bronco in a rodeo.

She hadn't seen much of him during the preparations for the wedding. He'd been busy at the ranch. She'd volunteered to take Lass home with her the nights his work kept him late.

Now they were a family.

Smoothing the satin skirt of her dress, she thought of the night ahead. The sun was setting. Soon it would be dark.

"Here we are," Sam said, bringing her out of her mood.

Tension knotted her stomach.

"I'll pull into the garage later. You might snag your dress." He paused, then added, "You were very beautiful today. You are beautiful. I know you don't think so, but . . . you are."

His words warmed her clear through. "Thank you," she managed to murmur. Honestly, she'd never get through the evening if every little thing got her all choked up.

She fumbled with the door and finally got out. Sam lifted Lass, car seat and all, and carried her into the house, motioning for Molly to go first.

The ranch house seemed warm and welcoming. She hadn't moved any of her things from her house yet, but she had plans.

Sam had surprised her by inviting her family out for a dinner of grilled chicken and a bakery pie for dessert the previous night. She'd made a salad and twice-baked potatoes to complete the meal.

Her suitcases were stored in the trunk of the car. Next week she would get the rest of her clothing and decide exactly what furniture she wanted to move. And there were all her dishes, linens, pots and pans plus the collected treasures of ten years to consider.

The church had already asked to rent her cottage for their caretaker and grounds keeper. She'd agreed, but asked for a month to sort through her stuff. At the moment, following Sam into her new home, her thoughts were too distracted to consider the furnishings.

"Let's get Lass settled, then I'd like to change," she told him. She wondered what brides wore in the interim between the wedding and preparing for bed. A going-away suit hardly seemed appropriate since she was already at her destination.

The new sports outfit she'd bought last month, she decided. It was a soft knit the color of spring grass with eyelets embroidered in gold and rust-colored satin thread.

"Right. I'll bring your luggage in."

She watched as he headed back outside in a long stride. She wondered if he felt as awkward as she did. There'd been no more torrid sessions like the night in her kitchen. Sam had been almost rigidly circumspect after that.

A niggling fear that she expected more of this marriage than she was going to get nagged her. No words of love had been spoken by either of them. Kisses had been brief and very few.

Had he married her only to protect Lass and save his land from his father-in-law? No. She couldn't believe that after the passionate interlude they'd shared.

Memories of those kisses had haunted her dreams. This moment might have been easier if they'd already become lovers, she thought, standing awkwardly in the middle of the living room.

Lass stirred and whimpered slightly. Molly carried her to the bedroom and put her in the crib. Lass smiled up at her, then promptly closed her eyes, pulled a corner of the blanket around her thumb and stuck it in her mouth.

The sleep of the innocent, Molly mused, gazing at the child with a heart filled with love. Hearing Sam's footsteps in the hall, she stiffened. Clutching the billowing skirt of her dress, which had been her mother's and grandmother's before her, she rushed out and closed the nursery door behind her.

"Lass asleep?" he asked.

She nodded.

"She'll probably be out for the night. It was a long day, and she didn't have a nap this afternoon."

They stood there for a minute. The silence intensified. Only the night-lights were on in the hall. They were a foot from the polished stone floor, shaded by a clever adobe awning that was part of the wall. The effect was one of semicircles of light along the hallway.

"Your room is this way," Sam finally said. Heat slid down and pooled in the lower part of his body. He wasn't sure he could keep his vow to give her time to adjust to him and decide if she really wanted this marriage. But he had to. He had to play fair with Molly.

She followed behind him. He opened a door at the end of the hall and on the opposite side from Lass's room. It was a neat room with Spanish oak furniture—an ornate bedstead and matching dresser. Two chairs and a table formed a sitting area.

"This is a guest room," she said.

He saw the puzzlement on her face. He set her two pieces of luggage on a bench at the end of the bed and rubbed his hands down his thighs. He felt sweaty-palmed and as awkward as an adolescent on his first date.

"Molly," he began. The room was lit only by the sunset. It felt too dark, too intimate. He flicked the wall switch and two lamps beamed pools of light, one on the bed, the other on the table. "Listen, we don't have to begin our marriage right away. I realize I sort of forced you into it."

He stopped, unable to explain that he valued her friendship, that he was afraid she'd dislike his love-making. She was a lady, and sex was... well, it could be sort of wild.

She said nothing. Just stood there watching him.

He felt a prickle of misgivings, but having started he had to finish. "Later, if you want an annulment, if you find ranch life boring, well, it would be easier all around if things were kept... simple."

"Simple," she repeated.

"Yeah." He didn't like the look in her eye. The satin moved over her breasts, then stopped. He realized she'd taken a deep breath and was holding it. He stared, fascinated, until the material moved again, slowly, deeply... again, then again.

"And in the meantime, I'm to be a guest here?" Her voice was deadly quiet.

Sweat popped out on his forehead. "For your sake, I thought it would be best."

"Because you think I'll grow bored and want to leave." She finished the thought for him. "Is that what your first wife did?"

"Yes."

He was pretty sure he'd made a bad mistake in not explaining all this before the wedding. Molly's mouth primmed up and her stance subtly shifted. Flags of color flew in her cheeks.

If he didn't know her better—that she was a sensible, levelheaded woman—he'd have thought she was furious.

"So we're to have a trial run before we commit ourselves?"

Put like that, it sounded pretty silly. "Well, yes. I think that would be reasonable."

He tried to explain, to show her he was being gallant about it, that he wouldn't expect more than she wanted to give—

She gave him a look that would have stopped a charging buffalo, much less his stumbling, rambling explanation, and walked to the door.

"How long do you think it will take before everyone in the county knows we're sleeping in separate rooms?" she questioned. "Then they'll really have something to talk about."

She left the room. He heard a door slam. She'd left the house. He hurried after her, wondering how to make things right when every word he'd uttered had made them more and more wrong.

Molly gripped the top rail of the fence with both hands. Anger burned hot and bright within her. She couldn't figure anything out, not Sam, not their hasty marriage, nothing.

Except he didn't really want her.

He had made her think they were in love. Those kisses in her kitchen, he had wanted her then. However, she was old enough to know that sex didn't mean love. As of this moment, she hadn't a notion of what it *did* mean.

Across the paddock, a big red horse eyed her, then snorted a couple of times. He threw up his head and neighed.

Molly gave him her teacher's stare. His racket interfered with her thinking. She pressed a hand to her temple, causing the ruffles of Brussels lace at her sleeve to cascade down to her elbow. Thunder rumbled. She glanced up in surprise.

The horse charged toward her. She moved back a step and watched it in a disinterested fashion. It came right up to the fence and stopped, then, arching its neck over the rail, it tried to bite her!

She slapped it on the nose, then was appalled. She'd never touched another living thing in anger before.

It threw up its head and screamed, then ran around the paddock kicking its rear legs up in the air like a ninny.

Molly leaned on the rail. "Stop that," she ordered. "You look silly." She snatched a clump of succulent grass from beside a boulder and held it over the rail. "Here, you spoilt bully."

The big red monster quit its act and watched her from a distance. Finally it began to sidle over that way.

From the shadows of the back patio, Sam shook his head at the two cowhands who'd come out of the barn to see what the ruckus was about. One held a lariat in his hand. The other held a pitchfork ready to drive the stallion back if necessary.

Sam watched as the stallion, known as a man hater, edged closer to Molly's outstretched hand. He wanted to grab her and shield her from danger, but was afraid to move, afraid he'd startle the red into more of a fury.

"Molly," he called softly. "Move back. That horse is dangerous. He hates people."

She didn't show that she'd heard his words, just continued to stand there. On the night air, he heard her murmuring voice calming the big horse. To his amazement, the horse reached out and took the tuft of grass. Then Molly stroked its neck and ran her fingers through its forelock.

When the stallion snorted and galloped to the far side of the paddock, Sam ran across the yard and grabbed Molly away from the fence. "Don't ever disobey me again," he ordered.

"What will you do—beat me?" And she smiled up at him with all the insolence of the boy he'd once been, bent on defying his stepfather and running the ranch the way his father had.

"Don't tempt me," he advised and knew from the flare of anger in her eyes that she'd drawn a battle line between them.

"Ah, hell," he said and hoisted her into his arms.

Startled, she clutched his shoulders. "What are you doing?"

"Taking you to bed."

Molly burned with humiliation as Sam carted her toward the house. Behind them, she could hear laughter as well as shouts of encouragement from the two cowboys who were helping out on the ranch that summer.

She felt utterly ridiculous—the plain-Jane who had naively thought this dashing, handsome man was in love with her. How could she have been so stupid?

Her foolish heart had read more into the situation than had been there. She'd been too inexperienced to understand.

"Put me down at once," she ordered in a voice sure to bring the desired action in the classroom.

He ignored her. Sam Frazier wasn't a four-year-old used to obeying the teacher. He carried her into the house and into a suite of rooms that opened off the living room.

After setting her down on the carpet beside the bed, he caught her arms. When she struggled, he simply held on, his thumb and fingers encircling her wrist, not hurting, but holding her securely.

She realized the futility of trying to break his hold. "If you think I'll…I'll…*cohabitate* with you after that insult, I can tell you right now—I won't."

"What insult?" He looked thoroughly puzzled.

He didn't even know! She certainly wasn't about to enlighten him on her lovelorn expectations.

"I was thinking of you and your comfort," he said impatiently. "I know you haven't slept with a man—"

She couldn't control the gasp, nor the heat that rushed into her face. "You can't tell," she began, then stopped, uncertain.

His knowledge of the female body exceeded hers on certain subjects. Another humiliation. She gave him a fulminating glance, crossed her arms over her chest and stared out the window at the cactus and sage growing on a nearby hill.

Sediments of the multicolored silt that had once covered the floor of an inland sea were exposed by erosion, forming layered hues of rusty red and ocher and tan over the terrain. She stared at the hill until the colors blurred and she had to blink.

"Look, I'm not asking you to cohabitate." His very tone mocked the word and her use of it. He knew very well what she meant. "You were the one who brought up what people would think about us having separate rooms. You're right. No matter how careful we are, things have a way of getting out."

She rounded on him, words rushing so sharply to her tongue she had to bite them back. To say them would be to admit her fantasy that he'd fallen in love as she had. Pride wouldn't allow her to concede that much to him. "I'd rather sleep with a rattlesnake," she said instead.

"You'll sleep with me," he snapped. "And like it."

"I will not!"

A weary smile hovered at the corners of his mouth. "Well, maybe you won't like it, but you'll sleep in this bed. And I probably won't sleep at all," he added with a smile dipped in acid and stalked out the door.

She stood in the too-silent room and wondered what she should do now. Going to the window, she watched the long shadows of evening color the mesa lavender and magenta and purple.

Diablo Mesa. The Devil's land. And she was going to be sleeping in his bed!

A thump outside the door brought her heart to her throat. Sam brought her bags in, placed them none too gently on the floor and walked out without saying a word.

She pushed the door closed and laid her hand on the lock.

* * *

Sam's headache rose a notch at the slam of the door behind him. He sighed. There were chores to be done. He grimaced at his suit. Damn. He went out to the barn anyway.

Sandy and Tom were mucking out the stables. He nodded to them and grabbed a bucket. After putting it in the stallion's manger, he eased the outside door open, then quickly retreated, getting the stall door closed before the big horse could come inside and try to kick him into oblivion.

Although he could use a little oblivion right now.

He leaned on the stall gate and watched the red come tearing inside and dip his nose into the oats.

It was a fact, he'd never understand women. Here he'd tried to be gentle and patient with Molly, considerate of her feelings and all, and what had happened? She'd gotten huffed up like a puff adder and nearly taken his head off.

Hell, he should have just taken her to bed and done all the things he wanted to do to her. That would show her.

But, he reasoned, he was trying to be fair to her. Dammit, he was trying to act like an honorable man rather than a rutting stag crazy with lust.

He knew Molly wasn't the spoiled prima donna his wife had been, but she might not like ranch living. She might not like *him* once she got to know him. However, he had to convince her to stay with him for a year. Maybe by then everyone would forget or disregard any rumors spread by Tisdale.

The big red threw up his head and whickered for more oats when he finished. Sam glared at the animal.

"Hey, boss, watch out for that man hater," Sandy called, stopping work to lean on the pitchfork and toss a grin his way.

"Yeah. He's a mean'un all right," Tom agreed, coming out of a stall after spreading clean straw. "Won't let a man within a hundred feet, but now gals is a different story. B'lieve the red has a soft spot for pretty little fillies."

"Yep," Sandy chimed in. "She walked right in and wrapped the meanest bronco this side of the Pecos around her finger. Think the boss eats out of her hand, too?"

The two cowboys laughed uproariously at their humor. Sam gave them a narrow-eyed glare, then grinned, too. An idea came to him. "Hey, you may be right. The red might take to a human female."

The rope burns on the mustang's neck testified to his misuse at the hands of the men who'd tried to catch and tame him. It had been a stroke of pure luck that the red had entered an open paddock when the men were moving the remuda. The big mustang had been after his mares.

Sam saw the men had the chores well in hand. He headed for the house. He had other fences to mend.

He entered the kitchen cautiously. No pot hurled past his head the way it once had.

Molly wasn't there. He hurried down the hall, worried that his bride might decide she didn't want to stay even one night on the ranch. After checking on Lass, who was out for the night, he silently tried the doorknob to his room. It turned.

He was grateful for small favors. At least she hadn't locked him out. "Molly?"

No answer.

She wasn't in the room. Her luggage was gone. He whirled around, intending to go down the hall and get her. A noise from the adjoining room stopped him. Opening the door, he saw her.

As if he weren't there, she calmly hung a dress in the closet. She had changed from the wedding gown to a pants and top outfit. He couldn't help but notice how nicely curved she was.

"What are you doing?" he asked after clearing his throat.

"Unpacking." Her face, usually so open, was closed.

"In here?"

"Yes."

The room reflected the tradition of the past century when a smaller room commonly adjoined the master suite. It had been used as a nursery in the past. His mother had used it as a sitting room where she read and sometimes entertained close friends.

It had a daybed against one wall. A Greek recliner and two comfortable rockers along with a dressing table and three smaller tables completed the furnishings.

"Then you're going to stay?"

She gave him that drop-dead glance again. "Of course. Our marriage has hardly begun." She placed the hanger in the closet, closed her empty suitcase and placed it inside before closing the closet door.

For a second, she stood there as if thinking, then she looked him square in the face. "Did I tell you I don't believe in divorce?"

Relief washed over him. "No."

"I don't."

"All right." Whatever she wanted, he was agreeable. If she'd left before the first day was over...God, he wouldn't live that down in two lifetimes.

He didn't like the idea of marriage, but he liked Molly. If ever a marriage had a chance, it should be this one. Without the confusing issue of love, which was a nice name for lust, they'd get along fine. They'd be friends, then they could be lovers.

But he wouldn't rush her. He'd control his impulses. He'd show her how much fun life on the ranch could be.

A sinking sensation hit his middle. He'd tried that once. But Molly was different. She was interested in all kinds of things—the land, history, people, weather, everything. She was a woman a man could talk to.

Except she didn't seem to be speaking to him at the present.

She walked across the room. He moved aside, then followed her down the hall to the kitchen. She opened the refrigerator.

"I'm hungry. Do you want a sandwich?" she asked.

"Yes." A question burned in the back of his mind. "If you don't believe in divorce, how long are you going to stay in the other room?"

"Until the time is right."

Chapter Seven

Sam turned on his side, lay there, then flipped over to the other side. He settled on his back and stared at the patterns of moonlight on the ceiling.

He'd go for a hell-for-leather ride, but sure as he did, the ranch hands would wake and think it was a rustling operation. That's all he needed—for them to come running out, loaded for bear, and find him restless and unable to sleep.

Hell.

He'd never been in a fix like this before. He was acutely aware that through the door separating the bedroom from the sitting room was his wife. Once he'd heard her cough. That had been soon after they'd eaten their sandwiches—their wedding supper—and she'd gone to her room, saying she was tired.

After that, he'd heard her in the bathroom, then she'd disappeared for the rest of the evening. He'd watched TV until ten, then he'd gone to bed. And here he lay.

One o'clock.

Dawn came early on the ranch. They had a bunch of calves to brand, the one part of the operation he didn't like. But it had to be done before he turned them loose on the hilly range that formed the backside of the ranch. If his cattle strayed over on Tisdale land or vice versa, he didn't want any questions about which ones belonged to whose ranch.

He wondered what Molly had meant by that "until the time is right" remark. When would that be?

Marriage. It made him nervous. The female mind was beyond him. Elise had claimed to love him, but she'd hated being tied down, being pregnant. In the end, she'd hated him.

He didn't want the same to happen to him and Molly.

His body reared up at a sound...no, it was a coyote baying at the moon. Molly wasn't going to come waltzing in and climb into bed and...

Gritting his teeth, he forced himself to count backward from a hundred. Finally he fell thankfully into slumber.

Sunlight and the rush of running water awakened him the next morning. He lay there and listened while Molly took a shower. He wondered how she'd react if he joined her.

The pure pleasure of the thought entertained and tortured him until she finished. When he heard the door open, he didn't know whether to pretend to be asleep or not. Too late. She was in the room. Her eyes met his.

She paused. "Sorry, I didn't mean to awaken you."

She wore a robe of pink silky looking stuff with pink scuffs on her feet. Her hair was twigged on top of her head. She walked through the bedroom and into her room as if she were out for a Sunday stroll.

A grin pushed its way onto his mouth. Bet if he checked her pulse, the little schoolmarm's heart was beating like sixty. The way it had Saturday night three weeks ago...

At the clenching in his lower body, he dropped the thought and flung out of bed. In the bathroom, he paused before stepping into the shower.

Her scent lingered on the warm, steamy air. Two new toothbrushes had joined his in the toothbrush holder. A box of curlers, the kind that plugged in and heated up, sat at the end of the counter next to the wall.

A damp towel and washcloth hung neatly across the bath towel rack. A new bar of clear soap was in the soap dish. He lifted it and took a sniff. It had that fresh, clean scent he associated with her.

For the first time in days, he relaxed. They'd work their way through this marriage business. Molly was sensible. As soon as she got used to the idea, things would settle down. Then, when the time was right...

Molly prepared biscuits, ham and country gravy, which she'd learned to make since living in the west. It was an odd dish that cowboys, whether they were real or urban, seemed to relish. Made of bacon, sausage or ham drippings, thickened with flour like a white sauce, and milk, it was easy enough to prepare.

Except she replaced half the grease with vegetable oil to cut down on the saturated fat.

When Sam entered the kitchen, she ignored her wildly pounding heart and assumed a serene expression. She'd be so calm, so sweet, it would drive him nuts. "Breakfast will be ready in about ten minutes. Tell the men not to be late. I don't want the gravy to get cold."

"Uh, sure." He fairly rushed out the door.

She smiled grimly. Marriage was going to take some getting used to... for both of them. She'd learned the men usually ate together, taking turns with the cooking. She had some ideas along those lines to share with them.

Begin as you mean to go on.

Good advice for anyone starting on a new adventure. And marriage was surely that. Thus far it had been full of twists and surprises. She had a few twists of her own.

When she heard a cry from the baby's room, she turned off the burner, checked the biscuits in the oven, then hurried down the hall. Lass had pulled herself up at the side of the crib and was hollering for attention. She hushed as soon as Molly came in. Holding her arms up, she demanded to be held.

Molly cuddled her new daughter for a moment, the anger inside her softening slightly, then changed the baby's clothing before returning to the kitchen. After placing the child in the high chair with a toast triangle to chew on, she poured up the gravy and finished preparing breakfast.

When the men shuffled into the kitchen, she welcomed them with a cheery, "Good morning. Have you washed up?"

She saw that they had. The two ranch hands, whom she'd met briefly the previous week, had wet and slicked back their hair. The tooth marks from the comb were visible. They carried their hats in front of them like shields. She could see the dip in their hair where the hats usually rested.

Like Sam, they dressed in jeans, scuffed boots and work shirts. Their wiry grace fascinated her. Two stereotypical characteristics impressed her. They were as tough as whip leather, and they were shy.

"Please take your seats, gentlemen. Breakfast is ready." She moved Lass closer to the table.

After placing the basket of biscuits on the table, she took her place at one end and looked over the table with a critical eye. Frankly it looked delightful. Her mother would have been proud of her.

A green vase held some dried seed heads of a lovely golden hue. She'd found them along the fence row near the stable. The green-and-white striped place mats went well with the dishes, which were white with a dried wheat pattern along the edge.

The bowl of scrambled eggs, the platter of ham and the dish of gravy provided a nice contrast in color and texture. She took a biscuit and passed the basket along, then spooned some egg onto her plate. The men sat after she did and dug in.

For several minutes the muted sounds of forks against plates were the only noise. Molly observed with mounting awe the amount of food three men could put away in a short time. Amazement gave way to irritation when they ate without speaking.

"The past week has been lovely," she remarked to no one in particular. "I hope it bodes well for the rest of spring." She waited for a response.

The cowboy named Sandy broke open another biscuit—his third—and spooned gravy over the two halves. He forked another slice of ham onto his plate.

Tom sprinkled a generous helping of pepper over a second mound of perfectly cooked eggs. He slathered margarine on a biscuit, added a thick layer of jam, heaped a fluffy clump of egg on the edge of the biscuit and chomped it off with a look of pure delight on his face. His jaws worked vigorously.

Both men were in their mid to late twenties. Old enough to have manners.

Down the length of the table, Sam ate as silently, although not as voraciously, as his men. Her irritation doubled.

"Do you get to rest on Sundays, or do you have work that can't wait a day?" she inquired, maintaining an even tone.

Chomp, chomp.

She took a deep breath—

"Gentlemen, my wife expects people to answer when spoken to," Sam informed them. "We are civilized folks, aren't we?"

She saw the sardonic humor in his eyes before she quickly looked away. Was he making fun of her?

Anger and confusion roiled in her. She intensely disliked both feelings.

The two men stopped stuffing their faces and stared at her in the manner of startled bucks, not sure whether to bolt or not in the face of this possible, but unknown, danger.

Molly crimped her lips together to keep from saying something hateful. She reminded herself that indeed civilized people did not resort to shouting and insults.

Sandy's ears turned red. "Uh, we have some chores."

"But we have most of the day off," Tom offered. He held a half-eaten biscuit in his hand. He looked at it in longing.

Molly thought if he ever looked at a girl that way, he'd melt her heart like sun on snow. Her own heart softened. She'd tame these wild broncos in time.

All of them, she vowed, looking at her husband, who watched her with a moody stare while he ate.

Nodding, she ate her meal, allowing the men to do the same.

Lass clicked her tongue and waved her hand toward the table, wanting the adult food. Before Molly could rise, Sam was on his feet. He prepared jars of cereal and fruit.

"I'll feed her," he said.

Lifting the high chair, he placed Lass close to him and began feeding her, his expression serious as he concentrated on the task. Lass ate until her hunger was satisfied, then she started flirting with her father.

After getting no more than a preoccupied smile from him, she enlarged her scope to include the other two men. Sandy winked at her when she clicked at him.

"Ah, Lass has made a conquest," Molly teased, detecting a soft spot in the men's hearts.

"She's a heartbreaker, this one," Sandy agreed. He nodded his head toward his plate. "Appreciate the grub. I ain't had nothing this good since I got out of the army five years ago." His ears turned red again.

"It's kind of you to say so." She gave him her teacher smile that complimented a student who'd done well.

Sam wiped Lass's hands and face. "Last week he said my beef stew was the best he'd ever eaten."

"Well, it was pretty good," Sandy admitted. "First time you hadn't burned it."

The two cowhands laughed. Sam smiled.

Molly thawed somewhat. Her husband was a very handsome man when he stopped scowling at the world. She'd see that he smiled more often. It was one of several changes she intended to make in his life.

She struggled with anger while she wondered at the real reasons for their marriage. To protect her good name?

He'd been furious at the gossip about them and felt he'd caused it he'd said in that insulting explanation he'd made.

He had, but it took two to tango, as the saying went. If she'd been seen in his arms, she was as much to blame as he was. She had been as lost in that kiss as he had. More so, if the truth be known. She hadn't wanted to stop.

She wanted that mad, breathless passion again. She also wanted declarations of undying love. But it was obvious she wasn't going to get either of her wishes.

All night she'd tried to sort through things, but it had been hopeless. She didn't feel calm and logical. For one of the few times in her life, she wanted to shout and throw things. It was an insight into herself that wasn't pretty. It even shocked her a little.

Most of all, she felt cheated. She'd waited for years for the right man, well, not exactly waited . . .

Actually she hadn't thought much about marriage at all—she'd been busy establishing her school—then to have all these strange longings awakened by this one man was humiliating. He was her husband, but he didn't want to be.

There. That was the one insulting, inescapable fact she'd had to face during the long, black night.

It made her angry. It made her want to scream at him and demand to know why they'd married.

Protect her name? As if she needed someone to do that for her. She was a responsible human being and a darn good nursery schoolteacher. Her reputation was impeccable. Those who didn't think so were welcome to think whatever they liked.

She hadn't asked to fall in love, hadn't dreamed of finding someone she'd want to share the intimacies of marriage with. It was patentedly unfair.

Noticing Sam staring at her over his coffee cup as he drank, she jerked and nearly dropped her own cup. She glared at him.

He continued to study her. He looked as perplexed as she'd been when he'd taken her to the guest room.

The oaf. He hadn't a clue as to why she'd felt insulted by his supposed reason for wedding her.

To have one's dreams flung back in one's face, to find a love she hadn't expected, hadn't asked for, and realize it meant nothing, to be rushed into a marriage and find it wasn't a marriage... She couldn't bear thinking about it.

She clenched the cup as anger rolled through her once more. Maybe she didn't understand all the motives behind this ill-conceived merger, but she wasn't going to walk out.

Sam had married his first wife in the heat of the moment, so to speak. It had not turned into a happy union. Now he was married again, forced into it by his strong protective instincts, which no one seemed to notice but her.

However, she wasn't completely naive about the male-female relationship. There was a physical attraction between them. She suspected he was a sensuous, earthy man. To her amazement, she'd found she was something of the same.

With his first marriage, there had been nothing behind the passion. With her, Sam had a friend.

They both loved Lass and this harsh, beautiful country. Sam had seemed to enjoy her company during the month prior to his proposal. Having seen his love for his daughter, she knew he was a good man, capable of deep caring.

A flicker of hope overlapped the doubts. Maybe, just maybe, this marriage had a chance after all.

But on her terms, not his.

She lifted her gaze from her cup and gave him stare for stare. Luckily the two cowhands kept eating and didn't notice the tension between the boss and his lady...partner, she corrected. She took a deep breath. It was wise to have a plan.

Molly, the ever sensible.

"That was very good," her husband said when he finished.

He looked every inch the boss of the outfit. He'd been wearing a denim jacket when he came in. He'd hung it on a hook by the back door along with his hat. The other men had done the same. All three were at home on this rugged land.

She was the outsider here. She'd have to make a place for herself on the ranch as she had in the town. Summoning a smile, she responded to the compliment. "Thank you."

"Let's go, you guys. If you eat much more, you won't be worth a plug nickel the rest of the day."

He stood. So did Tom. Sandy wolfed down a last bite of biscuit with jam, then joined them.

"Be sure to rinse your plates before you put them in the dishwasher," she reminded them, starting her *begin as you mean to go on* plan with a sweet smile. "I'll clean up the rest of the kitchen this time. Next weekend, we'll take turns as usual."

There was a beat of hesitation, then Sam took his plate to the sink, rinsed it and put it in the dishwasher. The two cowboys followed his lead.

Finished, the three men grabbed their jackets and hats and left the kitchen.

"Good thing Sunday is a light day," Molly heard Tom say, loosening up once he was away from her inhibiting influence. "Did'ya notice Sam was moving kind'a slow this morning, Sandy? Half the chores were done before he showed up."

Molly felt a blush highlight her face. Sam's ears turned red. "Get on with it," he ordered gruffly, pausing before stepping off the porch. He returned to the kitchen. "Will you be okay here for a while?"

"Of course."

"I'll get the sides on the hay truck. We'll pick up some of the things at your house if you know what you want moved."

"I do." She laid her napkin aside and crossed the room. "What time will you be ready to go?"

"Around one." He glanced at the kitchen. "About lunch—"

"I have a roast started. On weekends, I usually prepare something that will last the first part of the week for leftovers and sandwiches."

"We can hire someone to help," he told her. "Someone could do the housework."

"I was thinking along those lines, too." She forced herself to nod agreeably. "I think we can work it out, don't you?"

Her question seemed to confuse him. "Uh, yes."

"I have a high school girl helping at the nursery in the afternoons. She has a friend who's interested, too. I think I'll hire them and ask Tiffany to close at night, so I'll get to the ranch earlier."

Sam stood there by the door, not wanting to leave the warmth and brightness of the house. He felt funny inside, sort of squeezed and anxious.

His new wife watched him without speaking. Her eyes were like curtains of mist this morning, obscuring her thoughts from him. He didn't like it. He wanted things as they'd been last month. All the world had seemed right then, as if things were finally going to go his way.

She seemed to be waiting for him to finish and leave. It irritated him—that wall of calm she'd erected between them. He stalked toward her.

Her eyes opened wider, but she stood her ground when he came near. He recognized defiance in her stance. It surprised him.

But then, so had her fury yesterday. Maybe she wasn't as open and easy to read as he'd thought.

She lifted her chin and waited for him to speak. Talking wasn't what was on his mind. Gone were his good intentions, his restraint. In their place was a burning need to remind her she hadn't found him all that repulsive in the past. He took hold of her upper arms and pulled her toward him.

Then his conscience kicked in.

He tried to ignore it, but couldn't. With a sigh, he gave up and loosened his hold on Molly. Truthfully he wasn't certain what she thought of touching and all that.

However, she had been caught up in a sensual daze that night in her kitchen. Still, he didn't want to shock her. He'd have to keep a tight rein on things.

He bent down slowly, carefully, giving her time to withdraw. She stiffened, but she didn't move away. He brushed her lips with his.

Her mouth was warm and sweet. Longings that he hadn't felt since he'd left home to make his way in the world stirred in him. He wasn't sure what they were.

He lingered, wanting a response from her, but she simply stood still, as if waiting for him to finish so she could get on with her chores. He pressed harder. Her lips moved slightly.

Fighting the urge to haul her into his arms, he jerked his hat down firmly on his head and headed outside. A friend, he reminded himself. Not a lover. A friend.

"No, no, I'm sorry, but this isn't right. Let's move it back." Molly lifted her end of the table.

Sam hefted the other. They moved the heavy dropleaf table back to its original position. He waited for her next command.

She realized what the problem was. The sitting room in the master suite was the perfect place for Sam's desk, not the formal dining room. The modern computer furniture didn't fit in with the carved walnut set.

However, until she moved out of the room, Sam could hardly claim it for an office. And she wasn't moving out, not until something changed between them.

Until he wanted her for herself.

"Okay, that's it. You can escape back into the great outdoors," she said, maintaining the light tone she'd managed for the past six days.

She hesitated, then went to him, unsure of what she was going to do. The week had been a tense one. Even the two cowboys had sensed it as they helped move furniture from her cottage to the ranch house.

It was difficult to maintain a facade of happiness in the face of Tiffany's probing interest. And the pastor's wife. They were keeping an eye on her, watching for signs of trouble.

She wasn't going to confess her marriage was on the rocks before it had even sailed out of the harbor.

But one thing she'd resolved. Her husband was going to know she was there, a part of his life whether he wanted her or not. He'd tried to avoid her all week, getting up and out of the house before the sun rose each morning, appearing only for meals, then again at bedtime. It was like being married to a ghost.

That had to change. Going to him, she put a hand on his shoulder and leaned against his arm companionably, making no demands one way or another. Under the cambric shirt, she felt his muscles tense and hold.

There was an attraction, and she was going to make the most of it. She liked touching, she'd discovered. It hadn't been a momentary madness. She was more sensual than she'd known.

And if it drove him crazy, so much the better.

She took pleasure in the strength and warmth of his body. She liked his bigness and no longer felt intimidated by it. A man who could handle a child the way he handled Lass was no threat to a woman.

In their six days of marriage, she'd learned more about herself than Sam. One thing—she wasn't the

patient person she'd thought she was. A second thing—
she wasn't above using those feminine wiles she'd read
about on him.

Leaning into him, she let him take a bit of her
weight, knowing he could also feel the warmth of her
body along his side as she did his. Then she moved
away and let him go.

When he walked out without saying a word, she followed him. She went over to the paddock where the red
mustang munched on the few blades of grass that
pushed through the compacted soil. After gathering
several handfuls of grass, she leaned over the railing
and held it out to him. He lifted his head and tweaked
his ears toward her.

They stayed that way several minutes.

At last the stallion couldn't stand it. He ambled over
and sniffed at the offering. Finally he decided to eat it.

Molly held her hand flat so the horse didn't acci-
dentally chomp on a finger. When the grass was gone,
she wiped her hand on the side of her jeans.

"Here's a bucket of feed," Sam said, coming out of
the stable. "Hold it and let him eat from it." He
handed it to her and stepped back from the fence.

She did as directed. The big horse stuck his head in
the container and *whuffled* in delight. The sound of
corn and oats being cracked between strong teeth made
her a bit nervous.

The bucket was awkward and too heavy to hold over
the railing for long. Finally she climbed up two rails
and was able to lower her arms to a more comfortable
position.

"Hang the bucket over the post and stroke his
neck," Sam called softly.

She hung the wire handle over the support post. The stallion followed as if he were a trained pet. She gingerly touched its neck. The powerful muscles twitched. She flinched in nervous reaction, then tried again.

The horse hadn't allowed her to touch it since she'd swatted it on the nose, then fed it the grass to say she was sorry. The mustang had galloped to the far side each time she'd paused by the fence and talked to it. Now it stood still, listening to her voice while it ate.

Laying her hand flat on the beast's neck, she rubbed down to the shoulder, then did it again. Feeling bolder, she ran her fingers under the heavy mane and through the rough hair, smoothing out some of the tangles.

The stallion shook his head and rolled his eyes.

"That's enough," Sam told her. "He's getting nervous. The bucket's empty. Move slowly and bring it with you."

She unhooked the handle and lifted it to her side of the fence. She climbed down to the ground, then walked toward Sam. He was grinning as if she'd done something great. She did feel a bit cocky about her success.

When she stopped in front of him, he hooked an arm around her shoulders and took the bucket from her. "You're going to tame him yet," he exclaimed exultantly.

Their eyes met. The smiles of triumph disappeared.

They stopped outside the stable door. Around them, tree frogs and crickets sang to the coming night. To her, it seemed like a love song. A shiver chased over her.

"It's getting cold," Sam murmured, his gaze on her mouth. "You'd better go in. We'll be ready to eat in a half hour."

She nodded. They lingered in the twilight.

Slowly he bent his head. Her breath came out in a shaky sigh. *Begin as you mean to go on.* She raised one hand and touched his cheek. Very gently. As if he were the stallion that needed taming.

She saw desire flame in his eyes and felt an answer in herself, that slow-fast buildup of heat and longing. His muscles bunched and she waited for him to take action.

For a heart-stopping moment, she thought he might overrule caution and carry her inside as he'd done that first night, but he simply heaved a deep breath and let her go.

It was extremely frustrating. If he wanted her, why had he insisted they needed time to get to know each other?

She went inside to see if Lass was awake. She was.

"Hi, fussy thing," she said with a sympathetic smile at the child when she went into the bedroom and flicked on the light.

The baby was teething. Top and bottom teeth were erupting almost simultaneously. Lass was irritable. Her sleeping habits had become unpredictable. They had hardly slept two hours in a single span for the last four nights.

Molly decided she'd give the child some baby pain reliever when she went to bed for the night. "Come on, we'll have some dinner before Da-da and the men have theirs." She lifted Lass from the crib and carried her to the kitchen.

When Sam and the cowboys came in, Lass had more food on her and the high chair than in her tummy. She whimpered and waved her arms on seeing her father, knocking the spoon from Molly's hand and sending pureed apples across Molly's shirt and the floor, which had already been mopped twice that day.

Her success with the horse wasn't being repeated with the child. Lass was as cross as a sore-tailed coyote and didn't want anything to do with her.

"I'll take care of it," Sam said. He swiped up the floor with a damp paper towel. He handed another one to Molly after glancing at the apples sprayed across her chest.

While she wiped her shirt, Sam worked on Lass, getting most of her supper down her by teasing and playing with her.

Molly felt the foolish press of tears. She had set the table when the two ranch hands came in, washed and ready for the meal. Five minutes later, they sat down to eat.

When Lass started crying, she sprang to her feet, but Sam was already up. He held Lass and paced the floor while Molly and the men ate.

"Getting hot now," Tom told her. "The hay is coming along. We'll be able to cut the first lot by the end of May if the weather stays this warm."

She'd asked so many questions about ranching that the men, especially Tom, who she suspected was a little sweet on her, automatically filled her in on what they were doing and what was coming up. Sam scowled and said nothing.

When Sandy finished his meal, he took Lass and walked up and down the kitchen floor with her, keeping her quiet. When Molly finished, she took her turn.

Sam cleaned up the kitchen after sending the men to the bunkhouse for the night. Molly gave Lass a teething ring and put her in the high chair.

"You look tired," Sam commented.

She pushed a strand of loose hair out of her face. "I never realized what a blessing it is to send children home with their parents at the end of the day."

He nodded. "I thought I was going to lose my mind that first couple of months with Lass. She seemed to cry all the time. One night I couldn't stay awake any longer. I fell asleep in front of the TV. When I woke at dawn, I realized Lass had either slept all night or cried herself back to sleep if she woke up. At any rate, she slept all night from then on. It was a relief."

"I can imagine."

"She's been a good baby, otherwise."

"She's adorable, but it does make me anxious when she cries. I feel I have to do something for her right away. Being a parent isn't as easy as it sounds in the books."

"Ah," he drawled, "the wisdom of experience."

She smiled. Between rearranging her time and running the nursery school, getting herself and her personal items settled in the ranch house, and taking over some of the care of Lass and the house, she felt as tired as a new parent.

"I've found someone to do the housework," she told him.

"Who?"

"A Mrs. Stevens. She helps in the nursery at church sometimes. She's a widow."

"I don't know her." His face hardened. "You're not to let anyone around Lass without my approval."

She was dumbfounded by this order.

"Her grandfather—" He stopped abruptly.

"Surely you don't think Mr. Tisdale would try to kidnap her, do you? He couldn't possibly get away with it."

"I don't trust him. Lass isn't to be left alone with anyone at any time."

"I leave her with Tiffany at school when I have errands." She reminded him rather stiffly.

He frowned. "I guess that's all right. Make sure Tiffany knows not to go off and leave those teenagers in charge."

"The nursery is my responsibility. I'll handle my staff."

He started to say something more, something harsh she was sure, but he refrained. "Just make sure they know about Lass. No one, but no one, takes her anywhere but me or you."

"I'll see that they understand the rules."

"I..." He raked a hand through his hair, which was developing lighter streaks from his days in the sun. She'd often seen him with his hat and shirt hanging on a post while he worked at branding the calves, a task she couldn't watch.

"Yes?" she asked, coolness in her tone.

He sighed. "I'm sorry. I didn't mean... I know you'll watch over Lass."

"Did you ever think that you might win your former father-in-law to your side if you tried a different tactic with him?"

His scowl returned. "Like what?"

"Inviting him over to see Lass. Acting friendly. Making the first move. The flies and honey trick." She ended on a lighter note, seeing his frown deepen.

"There are some things that can't be changed," he told her in a voice like ice shards. "I don't want him near Lass." He caught her arm. "Don't try any of your schoolteacher tricks on him. They won't work."

She didn't say anything. His distrust of people rose like a wall between them.

Chapter Eight

"Are you sure you want to sign this?"

Sam nodded. He had no choice. "Yes."

His attorney gave a resigned shrug and pushed the document across the desk.

Picking up a pen, Sam flipped to the second page and signed his name on the line. Of all the uncertainties in his life, this wasn't one of them.

If anything happened to him, his wife, Molly Clelland Frazier, would inherit the ranch free and clear. She would also become a cotrustee of Lass's fortune, along with the lawyer and the bank.

He'd also given Molly his living power of attorney in case he became incapacitated for some reason.

"Are you going to let Molly adopt Lass?" Chuck asked.

Sam looked at him blankly.

"If she becomes Lass's legal mother and you two get a divorce, she'll have equal rights to custody." The attorney looked worried. "She might anyway."

"Molly doesn't believe in divorce."

"Yeah, and lightning doesn't strike twice in the same place." Chuck gave him a sharp glance, then picked up the will, looked it over and replaced it in the file folder. "Does she know she's your chief beneficiary, and that she holds the power of life and death over you?"

"Not yet."

"Maybe you'd better not tell her until you see how things go. You might change your mind. I've seen more than one man make serious mistakes in the throes of... uh, early marriage."

Sam didn't care for the cynical remarks. Besides, Chuck didn't know the half of it. Since there was no sex between them, he wasn't in danger of losing his mind because of it.

However, he might due to the lack of it.

Something had changed, but he didn't know what it was. If he hadn't known her better, he would swear Molly was acting the temptress. Only she was more subtle about it than any woman he'd ever known. There was something so naturally innocent about her. She couldn't have a conniving bone in her body.

But sometimes, when she looked at him in a certain way... Well, it stirred the blood and made him dream of nights with her in his arms. Sometimes he thought she did it deliberately.

No, he knew Molly. She wasn't a vamp. Neither was she out for the main chance. She had a comfortable nest egg put away, and her nursery earned a darn decent living. She didn't need anything from him.

"You were the one who told me to marry her," he reminded the other man.

Chuck gave him a severe look. "Yeah, but I didn't tell you to put your life and fortune in her hands."

"Who else have I got?" Sam pushed up from the chair and headed for the door. He paused before leaving and gave his friend a cynical grin. "My lawyer and banker? Most people would tell me to watch out for you two, not my wife."

Chuck snorted in disdain.

With a laugh, Sam went out, closing the door before the paper clip the attorney threw at him could land. He heard it plink against the wood. He nodded at the secretary, who was on the phone, and stepped out into the mild spring afternoon. The streets of Roswell were crowded with going-home traffic.

Hurrying now, he drove out the road toward the ranch, but that wasn't his destination. He'd decided to stop by the nursery and see if his girls were there.

His girls. Molly would probably deliver a lecture about the male possessive attitude and the reference to her as a girl, but that's the way he thought of her and Lass. They were his, and he dared anyone to try to take them from him.

Loosening his grip on the steering wheel, he considered the past seven days. It still gave him a pleasurable shock to come in at the end of a hard day and see the lights on at the house, to know they were there, waiting for him.

Molly and Lass and the two cats. His girls.

He turned off in front of the church and drove down the winding road to the nursery. Through the open curtains, he could see the children inside, all as busy as bees in a clover patch.

Molly was there, too. She was reading a book to several children gathered around her on the floor. Lass lay on a mat beside Molly. Another group of kids worked on some project with the other teacher at the back of the room.

As he watched, a knot formed in his chest. Breathing became difficult. The problem happened frequently of late. It worried him. He wasn't sure what it meant.

Shaking off the feeling, he climbed down from the truck and went into the colorful room. There were pictures of flowers everywhere, plus some real ones growing in pots around the room.

"Hello. Come join us," his wife invited. She moved over a space so he could sit on the cushion beside her. "We're almost finished with this story. Can someone tell Sam what has happened so far?"

Sam folded his legs in front of him and plopped down. He listened while six kids tried to tell him about the story.

"Okay, I got it," he said, recalling the story from his childhood days.

Molly called for quiet and began reading again.

Sam smiled at Lass. His daughter gave him a drooling grin, turned over on her stomach, bunched her knees under her and crawled into his lap.

"Oh, look, children," Molly exclaimed. "Lass has learned to crawl. Good girl, Lass."

The kids cheered and offered encouragement. Sam felt the squeezing sensation in his chest again. Inhaling deeply, he caught a whiff of Molly's soap and cologne. It was as familiar to him as the smell of his shaving soap.

She took a shower in the morning. He took one at night when he came in from the ranch work. He looked forward to Sunday. He'd like to linger in bed and listen to the sound of running water, his imagination steaming up his thoughts as he pictured her in the shower, which was roomy enough for two.

Fighting back the images this called forth, he lifted his daughter into a comfortable position. Lass made gurgling noises while Molly resumed reading.

When the story was over, Molly and the children talked about the tough choices the young hero of the tale had had to make. Sam realized the reading session was also a lesson on ethics.

"I'm ready to go. Are you heading for the ranch?" she asked him after she stood and dismissed the kids for a play period.

"I thought we might eat out tonight."

Her gaze drifted over him. He'd cleaned up before coming to town. Instead of jeans, he wore dress slacks. He'd even put on a tie with his white shirt. However, he'd drawn the line at adding a coat. The temperature was in the seventies, although the air would cool with the coming of night.

"That would be nice. I'll tell Tiffany I'm going."

While she told her assistant goodbye, he walked outside with Lass. They looked at a yellow lupine growing near the driveway.

"Da-da," Lass said and touched his face.

"She knows who you are," Molly said, coming up behind them, her purse and jacket in her hands.

She looked trim and stylish in green slacks with a white blouse striped in the same green. He'd noticed she wore pearl studs in her ears. She'd explained she didn't wear dangly earrings around the children. It was too easy to get one yanked out by accident.

On her left hand, she wore the wedding band and pearl ring that had been his mother's engagement ring. Tiny diamonds formed arcs around the pearl. It was an old-fashioned design. He'd offered to have it reset or to get something different, but Molly had been delighted with it.

Nine days and she still seemed pleased and interested in everything at the ranch. She and the cats. They, too, were curious about everything. Now that Molly let them outside—she hadn't the first week—they were as likely to appear in the stable as the house. One of them had taken a shine to Sandy.

Things were working out. He'd give Molly a couple more months, then see how she liked it. A cold, wet winter like the last one, slogging through the mud and muck to check on five hundred hungry cows, could change a person's romantic views real fast.

But there was no way he could wait until winter. She'd have to make up her mind about staying before then. He forgot the cynical advice when she stooped and studied the lupine with them.

"It's a pea flower," she said.

"Yes." He drew in the sweet essence of her. This close, he noticed the texture of her lips and the tiny scar that marred the perfect outline of one.

"Does that mean it's a legume?"

He didn't really hear the question. "Yes."

She stood. "I need to stop by the grocery store. Would you rather take Lass to the truck stop and wait there or go to the market with me?"

Standing, he lifted Lass into the air a couple of times while she squealed with delight. "We'll save you a seat at the restaurant."

"Now why did I think that would be your choice?" She smiled, gave Lass a kiss on the cheek, then left.

Sam watched her for a second before buckling Lass into the truck and heading toward the truck stop. It would be crowded on Friday night, which was good.

The few times he'd gone to town since the wedding, everyone from the bank teller to the guy at the gas station had asked how Molly was. He wanted the townsfolk, especially the gossips, to see their darling teacher so they'd know she'd survived the first seven days of marriage to him.

Molly squeezed into the parking place next to Sam's truck and hurried inside the restaurant. She spotted Sam and the baby easily. He was the best-looking man in the place.

She admitted she might be a little prejudiced in his favor, but he really was handsome. She slid into the other side of the booth. "Hi. I made it. Have you ordered?"

"No, I was waiting for you." He signaled the waitress after Molly looked over the menu.

The girl brought a cup of coffee for Molly and refreshed his cup. They gave their orders, then Molly suggested he give Lass some crackers and juice.

"Damn," Sam muttered under his breath.

She looked up in surprise. She'd rarely heard him use any swear words. She twisted around to see who he was watching.

It took a couple of seconds, but she connected a name with the faces. The older couple taking a seat at the one empty table in the place was Mr. and Mrs. Tisdale, Sam's former in-laws.

She observed Sam while he watched them. A grim frown etched a furrow between his eyebrows. He nodded his head toward them.

Glancing around, she saw the other two had seen them. It didn't take a genius to recognize the animosity between the two men. Mr. Tisdale was a large, beefy man, probably handsome in his younger days but running to fat now.

His wife was a tiny woman, so scrawny she reminded Molly of a wet cat. The woman was gazing their way like a starving person left out of a banquet. Molly realized it was Lass that held Mrs. Tisdale's gaze while her husband glared at Sam.

Her heart went out to the older woman. She settled in her seat. "You should take Lass to visit them," she told Sam. "Mrs. Tisdale is dying to know her granddaughter."

Sam flicked her a glance that warned her off.

She wasn't a person who could sit back and do nothing when she saw a situation that needed attention. "We could invite them over for dinner one night."

"Let it go, Molly. Tisdale better not set a foot on my land. He's liable to get it shot off. He feels the same about me, and I sure as hell am not going over there."

His tone was so cold, she was taken aback. "My gosh, I can't believe two men can be so stubborn."

"You don't know the half of it," he said with a sarcastic edge.

"That poor woman," Molly said in heartfelt sympathy, feeling a kinship with Sam's former mother-in-law.

Sam's snort mocked her feelings. She glared at him.

"I told her she could visit Lass at my place, but she has to come alone." He glared at her.

Lass made a snubbing sound, a sign that she was getting ready to wail to the high heavens.

"Now see what you've done. You've upset the baby." Molly crooned to Lass and played pat-a-cake until the tears dried up.

Sam prayed for patience. He didn't want to quarrel with Molly over his former in-laws. A quiet dinner with his wife and kid. Was that too much to ask?

Over Molly's head, he could see Tisdale glance his way once in a while. Besides marrying Elise and turning down an offer to merge the ranches into one operation with Tisdale the boss, Sam wondered what else he'd done to make Tisdale hate him.

The man reminded him of a trapped fox he'd once seen, its eyes cunning and desperate. He looked at Molly and Lass, worry eating at his insides. He'd do whatever was necessary to protect them. A fierce tenderness rushed over him. They were his, and he'd not let anyone hurt them.

When their food came, he tried to follow his wife's dictum for table manners. "How did things go today?"

She glanced at him with a preoccupied air, her thoughts obviously miles away. She was a quiet person, introspective and reflective in her nature. He wondered what she did alone in her room at night. She usually retired early.

"Fine," she said. "We're going to put on a play next weekend. We could use a hand with the props."

He'd never been much of a social mixer, but with her gaze on him, fully expecting him to volunteer and, more than that, to *enjoy* it, he couldn't refuse. "What do you need done?"

They talked about the play for the rest of the meal. He found himself agreeing to make a gingerbread house out of plywood for Hansel and Gretel to find. Watching Molly's face while she talked about the project, he wondered why he'd ever thought she was plain or prudish.

Enthusiasm sparkled in her eyes as they talked. Her smile was frequent and natural the way it had been before they married. A flush highlighted her cheeks.

He watched her lips move while she explained her plans for the event. He barely listened as she spoke of the social hour that would follow the play.

With those eyes like moonstones, that delicate complexion and little cat face, she was really very pretty. The difference between her and other women was that she didn't *act* pretty. She wasn't impressed by her own or other people's looks. She expected courtesy and decorum from people. And usually got it.

They finished just as Lass was getting cranky. He was relieved to be going. A squalling kid could make a nervous wreck out of a Tibetan monk.

Molly held Lass while he paid at the register. Carrying the baby seat, he took his wife's arm to guide her out. They had to go past the Tisdale table.

He knew what was going to happen. Molly dug in her heels and wouldn't be urged forward no matter how he tried to ease her past the older couple.

"Mr. and Mrs. Tisdale," she said cordially. She could drip honey when she wanted to, he noted. "I'm Molly Frazier, Sam's wife. Sam," she said sweetly, "look who's here."

She gave him one of her bright looks. He nodded. Her mouth screwed up. He forced out a "good evening," but she wasn't going to coax a smile out of him.

"And this is Lass," she continued as if they were all the best of friends. "I hope you'll come visit her soon."

"Oh, yes," Elsie said. She reached out. Lass grabbed her finger. "Oh, my, she's strong."

Sam was aware of the other diners avidly listening while pretending to eat their dinners.

"You can bring the child to visit us," Tisdale spoke up.

The light seeped out of his wife's eyes. She moved her hand away when Lass let go. "Perhaps we will visit," she said in a squeaky but stubborn voice. "One day."

Sam was surprised at the woman's spunk.

Molly beamed at them. "Good. We'll plan on it. If you have time, stop by the nursery. We're putting on a play next Friday. Hansel and Gretel. Do come if you have time. The children love to have guests to show off for."

With her usual warm manner, she said good-night to both the Tisdales and walked out. Sam heaved a sigh of relief. Tisdale was a dangerous man.

In the truck, he waited until Molly and Lass had pulled out onto the road, then followed behind them at a safe distance. He felt like a sheriff from the Old West, riding shotgun for a stagecoach of important passengers.

So he was. Molly and Lass were the two most important people in his life.

Molly drove in her usual careful manner, staying right on the speed limit. Sam usually drove about ten miles over, but fifty-five was fast enough on the highway. It was too fast when she turned off on the ranch road. She slowed to forty.

At the house, she parked in the garage while Sam left the pickup outside. He helped her carry in Lass and the groceries.

The two cowboys had been in and had supper, she assumed. She'd left a bag of homemade cookies on the counter with a note to take them to the bunkhouse with them. The bag was gone.

"I'll give Lass her bath," Sam volunteered when she started putting the groceries away.

She nodded. Her mind stayed on the scene at the restaurant. For some reason, she felt sorry for the Tisdales. She'd sensed resentment in the grandfather. Some people couldn't accept growing old. She thought he was one of them.

Elsie Tisdale had once been a very pretty woman, probably something like her daughter, but now she was as crinkly and dried as an oat husk. The longing in her eyes when she'd gazed at Lass had wrung Molly's heart.

Something was going to have to be done about that. It wasn't fair for Lass to miss out on having grandparents who lived practically next door.

She finished putting things away. Yawning, she stretched wearily and tried to decide what to do next. She should wash a load of clothes so they wouldn't pile up, but she was too tired.

Tomorrow, she thought. She'd get home early and do it then. Thank goodness Mrs. Stevens had agreed to take care of the house. With Lass fussy and not sleeping well, Molly didn't have the energy to think about the house, much less clean it.

There was something to be said for a tiny cottage, she continued the line of thought as she went to the bedroom.

Without thinking, she opened the door and walked in. She stopped on the threshold and stared.

Sam stood by the closet.

Naked.

She'd never seen a naked man before.

Not in person, only movies. And never like this.

Her mind had switched to slow motion. She could only think of one word or phrase at a time. She clutched her throat while tingles cascaded down her skin like spilled champagne.

He turned slowly and faced her. She couldn't tear her gaze from his magnificent form. He was fully, flagrantly erect.

A man for all seasons, she thought, forcing her gaze upward. She swallowed as her nerves knotted into a ball and lodged in her chest. Meeting Sam's eyes, she could only stand still while his eyes searched hers as if looking for something that only he knew.

"Excuse me," she said and lit out for her room, scooting inside and closing the door like a rabbit leaping into its hole.

She fell onto the Greek lounge, her legs trembling, her breath uneven and harsh, like a runner's at the finish line.

If she lived to be a hundred, she'd never forget. That powerful masculine image burned behind her eyelids. She couldn't close her eyes without seeing it...

Pressing her hands against her eyes, she tried to block out the shock and, she admitted, the pleasurable awe of seeing her husband without his clothes. She didn't think she could face him again. She'd blush, and he'd know what a ninny she was.

She heard his step outside the door and froze.

"I'm going to watch a program on TV," he called out. "If you need the bathroom, it's free."

"Thank you," she replied, sounding as stuffy as her mother had once said she was when she hadn't laughed at a guest's risqué story about the time he'd visited a nudist camp.

When she heard the outer door close, she changed to her pajamas and pulled on the matching robe and scuffs. As quick as a cat burglar, she finished her ablutions and returned to the safety of her room.

Once inside, she paced restlessly, then picked up a favorite novel she'd started reading over the weekend. She'd read it several times over the years. The story was a beautiful romance, one involving a teacher and a tough rancher. Two hours later, she finished the book and laid it on the table.

She compared her circumstances to those of the hero and heroine in the book. They'd known practically from the first moment that they loved each other. They'd stood by each other through all their troubles. That was the way love should be.

She didn't know what Sam wanted from her. He was her husband. She'd seen desire in his eyes that past week, but he held himself aloof, refusing even physical gratification.

He said they should wait until she was sure this was what she wanted, but she thought he was afraid of involvement.

Had his first marriage been awful?

Guiltily she repressed the surge of hope this thought produced. She'd never wish for happiness at another's expense.

She surveyed the titles of her beloved romance books. Some of them were marriage of convenience stories. She realized that was what she and Sam had. A marriage of convenience. It sounded feudal, medieval . . . Victorian at the very least.

And it was damn inconvenient as far as she was concerned!

This waiting was ridiculous. Making love was one of the most bonding of human endeavors. If more people realized that and paid attention to it in their marriages, the divorce rate would drop drastically.

Her mother had explained it. "A woman needs to feel loved to make love," she'd said. "A man needs to make love to feel loved. Make sure he feels loved. Tell him that you need to feel the same. Marriage is about two people giving and taking equally, not one doing all the giving while the other takes."

Molly believed that. It was the basis for friendship, too. Both had to get something from the relationship for it to last.

Now all she had to do was figure out a plan to make her husband overcome his scruples, or something like that.

Tomorrow she'd study on how to become a femme fatale.

Removing the many throw pillows from the daybed, she turned back the covers and slipped between the sheets. Every bone in her body sighed wearily. She fell asleep.

* * *

The wail seemed a part of her dream at first, then Molly realized it was Lass. She flicked on the lamp, leapt out of bed and dashed for the door. Sam had his light on when she entered his room. He paused by the bed and looked up.

This time she could only register his nakedness. She hadn't time to dwell on it. "I heard Lass," she said.

She went to the crying infant and lifted her into her arms. "There, darling, there now. Are those ol' teeth bothering you again? Poor baby."

Wiping the tears and runny nose with a tissue, she sat in the rocker and began to hum. Lass quietened and finally stuck her thumb in her mouth and laid her head on Molly's shoulder.

Sam entered carrying the medicine dropper. "Let's give her some of this. The pediatrician said it would help."

She held still while he gave the medicine to Lass, then began to rock again. Lass settled down, an occasional snuffle catching her breath.

Sam left with the medicine dropper. Molly heard him washing it in the kitchen. He returned in a minute and watched while she rocked and hummed to the baby, his shoulders propped against the doorframe.

After a while he pushed upright and crossed the room. "She's asleep now," he murmured.

He lifted the sleeping baby and deposited her in the crib. After covering her with a blanket, he patted her back, then motioned for Molly to leave when he went to the door.

Going down the hall, she realized she was in her pajamas, her feet bare. Sam was also barefoot. He'd pulled on a pair of jeans. The zipper hung open partway down his abdomen. She was acutely aware of this fact all at once.

"After midnight," he murmured. "Maybe she'll sleep until dawn. Do you have to go in early tomorrow?"

"Yes." It was hard to speak past the tightness in her throat. Their footsteps made hardly any sound on the Spanish tiles in the hall.

The entire house seemed to be holding its breath, waiting to see what would happen.

She wondered what Sam would do if she crawled into his bed. She regretted that she hadn't slept there when he'd carried her into the house on their wedding night. By now, their marriage would have been bonded in the most elemental way.

Sam was a sensual man, a man who took pleasure in using his body in his work. From his perceptiveness and gentleness, she knew he would be a considerate lover.

Her pride wouldn't let her stay with him that first time. Nor was she forward enough to suggest it now. Somehow he had to come to her, or at least meet her halfway, before this marriage would work. She'd have to make him see that.

In the meantime, there were those feminine wiles she needed to practice on.

Chapter Nine

Molly stirred the jar of baby food and set it on the desk before picking up Lass and putting her in the high chair. The other children were eating while they listened to a story being read by Tiffany.

After strapping Lass in and putting the tray across the chair, Molly took her seat and lifted the first bite toward Lass. The door to the nursery opened a crack.

A slice of face—an eye, part of a nose, mouth and chin—appeared in the one-inch opening.

"Come in," Molly called in a soft voice.

The door closed.

Puzzled, she went over and opened it. A woman stood on the other side. She looked so nervous, Molly was afraid she'd fall right over if someone said "boo" to her.

"Mrs. Tisdale," she said, putting extra warmth in her tone. "Please come in. We're having lunch. Won't you join us?"

While she chatted, she laid a hand on the other woman's arm and drew her inside. She closed the door behind them. "Come."

Mrs. Tisdale followed her to the desk at the side of the room. Lass waved her arms at the jars of food.

Molly had an inspiration. "She's hungry. Would you mind feeding her while I take care of our lunch?" She made this sound like a great favor.

As if in a daze, Mrs. Tisdale nodded her head. In less than a minute, Molly had the timid grandmother out of her suit jacket, an apron over her blouse and the spoon in her hand.

Molly headed for the kitchen. She prepared a plate of pasta salad and sliced vegetables for their guest. When she finished, she lingered and watched Mrs. Tisdale feed Lass.

The woman's hand shook noticeably at first, but she settled down after the first few bites. Lass, who hadn't yet entered her bashful phase around strangers, smiled and clicked while she ate the vegetables and fruit.

When the story was over, Molly helped Tiffany and the kids clean up the lunch debris, then it was quiet time. The children pushed the chairs out of the way and lay on their floor mats. The two teachers brought plates and drinks to the desk when the children were settled.

"It's time for Lass's nap," Molly said. "Tiffany, have you met Mrs. Tisdale?"

"Uh, no, I don't think so. That is, I don't think we were ever introduced." Tiffany cast Molly an uncertain glance before greeting the older woman.

"Please, call me Elsie."

"Sit here, Elsie," Molly invited, indicating the desk chair. "I'll tuck Lass in—"

"Oh, may I?"

Molly hesitated, recalling her husband's warning. Well, the woman was hardly going to grab the child and run off with her. "Of course. Do you want to change her diaper, or shall I?"

She led the way to the crib in the corner of the room, the sleepy Lass in her arms. After placing the baby in the bed, she laid the clean diaper out, along with a damp washcloth, and left Elsie Tisdale to do the work.

"I can't believe she's here," Tiffany whispered when Molly joined her at the desk. "I didn't know she knew how to drive."

"Maybe she had someone drop her off." Molly casually peered out the front window. "A late-model car is parked in the driveway."

"I've never seen her without her husband." Tiffany studied the woman as she fussed over her granddaughter. "He's a strange man. Elise used to fight with him something terrible. My dad said Mr. Tisdale has to control everyone around him. He hates anyone who doesn't agree with him."

"Maybe that's why he hates Sam," Molly mused aloud.

"Their quarrel was no secret. Mr. Tisdale wanted to combine the ranch operations after Sam and Elise were married, with himself giving the orders, of course. Sam declined the offer. Rumor has it Tisdale blew his stack and ordered Sam off his place after calling him a few choice names, ingrate the nicest among them, I understand."

"How foolish to alienate your family like that."

"Yeah. Apparently Tisdale suggested it in front of some men from the bank. I guess he was humiliated when Sam said no."

When Elsie finally finished with the baby, Molly told her she was delighted she'd decided to stop by. "A baby needs a sense of family," she told the woman. "I hope this won't be the last we see of you."

"It won't be," Elsie promised, her smile shy but pleased.

Molly's heart went out to the older woman. She wondered what her life had been like. Surely whatever love had been in it had disappeared when her daughter died. It wasn't right that Elsie be deprived of Lass because of her husband.

She was pretty sure that Mr. Tisdale didn't know his wife was visiting her granddaughter. Well, she and Tiffany were certainly not going to tell.

On the heels of that resolution came a question. How would Sam feel about it when he found out?

He said he'd given Elsie permission to visit her granddaughter. What if he'd changed his mind and didn't want Elsie around Lass, what would she do?

She'd see how things went. Maybe Elsie wouldn't get up the courage to return. If she did, Molly could explain it to Sam when she saw how grandmother and granddaughter got along.

Coward. She didn't want to deprive the woman of the baby, but she didn't want to face Sam's wrath when she defied him in case he said no to Elsie's visits. For defy him she would.

Elsie Tisdale needed something to nourish her soul, or the poor woman was going to dry up and blow away like a skinny tumbleweed during one of the wind storms. Lass, with her infinite supply of love, would be good for her grandmother.

A picture of her own dear grandmother, who'd given her a thousand shares of private family stock when she'd graduated from college, came to mind. Right now, Nana was on a cruise around the world or some such thing. Eighty-four and off on a lark.

Molly hoped she was as active and daring at that age. At any age, she added.

After they ate, Elsie quickly left, reminding the two teachers of a student who was afraid of missing the class bell.

"She's so timid," Tiffany said in a pitying tone.

"Do you think so?" Molly watched the car back, then pull forward and disappear up the winding driveway. "She came here even though her husband said she couldn't."

"When did he say that?"

Molly explained about the restaurant scene.

"He scares me." Tiffany shivered. "Anyone who hates that much and that long over something so silly, well, it scares me."

"Sam has left the ranch to me."

"He didn't!"

Molly nodded. "And the care of Lass."

Tiffany's mouth gaped. "He must really trust you to give you everything like that. It was said he put his lawyer in control of the ranch instead of Elise when they married and that the ranch was willed to the baby in case of his death. Elise supposedly threw a fit over it. I heard she'd already planned on divorcing him and taking him for all she could after the baby was born."

Molly couldn't hide her shock. What kind of people were these? She didn't want to know. The talk was making her uneasy, even though it was gossip.

"Well, let's see, we need to run through the play this afternoon. Can you work with Krissie on the song she's supposed to sing while I teach the bluebirds their dance?"

"Sure."

Molly put the problem of the Tisdales out of her mind.

Sam parked the truck near the barn. From the back, he hefted a calf and carried it inside. After putting it in a stall with clean straw to snuggle in, he trudged across the wide gravel driveway to his house.

The windows glowed like beacons. He'd seen them miles away and had followed them through the dark until he'd arrived home safe and sound.

Home.

Once he'd reached a point where he'd rather sleep in the stable than return to the house. No more.

Opening the back door, he inhaled the scent of stew, left on the back burner to cook slowly through the night. Molly was a miracle of organization. She planned and posted the weekly menus so he and the hands knew what to prepare if she didn't get home in time to start supper during the week.

The house looked nice in a sort of cluttered way. Molly might be organized, but she wasn't exceptionally neat. There were books and magazines on nearly every surface. Lists of things she'd planned were tacked all over the bulletin board.

He took off his boots and left them by the kitchen door. In sock feet, he went to his bedroom and shed his clothes, which were both muddy and bloody from birthing the calf he'd left in the barn. The mother hadn't made it.

He'd left the carcass in the field. The mountain cat living in the hills east of the ranch would find it. If not, the coyotes would. He wondered what Molly would think. She'd probably want to hold a wake and a formal funeral.

Grinning, almost groaning with weariness, he turned the shower on full blast and as hot as he could stand it. When he stepped out a few minutes later, he felt rejuvenated.

After drying and hanging up his towel—the schoolmarm didn't approve of wet towels left on the floor—he headed for bed.

The clock struck eleven. He paused by the window, yawning and stretching, and peered at the nightscape. The moon hung low and cast sooty shadows through the mesquite onto the rocks of the dry creek. A breeze flirted with the tree. The tree tossed its branches in a provocative response.

He thought of Molly's hair. It was softer than the down from the cottonwood trees that grew along the river. He tried not to, but sometimes he had to touch it... and then he'd think about how soft she would be all over.

Whew. That wasn't something to dwell on. Heat rippled through him, driving the fatigue from his muscles and bringing the clamor for relief from the fantasies he'd been having since their rushed marriage.

He couldn't deny it—he was on fire for his wife. Her scent, an article of clothing left in the bath, hell, anything and everything that was hers sent him into instant arousal. The way he was now.

Sighing, he folded the bedspread neatly at the end of the bed and pulled the sheet and blanket back. When he lay down, every muscle groaned. Except one. It was ready for action.

She'd been ready for him on their wedding night. He'd realized that later. He should have carried her to bed in the first place rather than trying to be so damn noble about rushing her.

God, he'd messed up. She'd been starry-eyed then and filled with expectations for their marriage.

He who hesitates is lost.

Yeah, well, he'd had good reasons to hesitate. He just couldn't remember what they were. Molly was the same person after marriage that she'd been before. She was still a lady and every inch a schoolmarm. With her disapproving stare and bright smiles, she could control an army.

Most important, she was still a friend. Other than those glances that sometimes made his blood heat up, she acted the same, listening and questioning until she understood all about the ranch and his concerns.

She told him about her school and her concerns, too. That reminded him, he had to load the gingerbread house on the truck and take it to town in the morning for the play tomorrow afternoon. He and the hands had worked on it every spare minute during the past two weeks. It looked nice, if he did say so.

He turned restlessly, then realized he hadn't eaten supper. He'd been too tired to think about it, wanting only a shower and bed. The aroma of the stew in the Crock-Pot had awakened his hunger. He tossed aside the cover, pulled on a pair of white briefs and headed for the kitchen.

Passing Lass's bedroom, he stopped and went in to take a quick peek at her. She was certainly happy with the new living arrangements. He paused on the threshold.

Molly was there.

She and Lass were asleep in the recliner-rocker she'd brought from her house in town. It was Molly-size, just right for her to snuggle in.

That odd, fierce tenderness he'd felt only for his child before Molly came into their lives clutched his chest. He couldn't put a name to it, but Molly invoked it just as Lass did.

It confused him to feel this way about a woman. He couldn't figure out what caused it. She wasn't a child needing his care and protection.

Bending, he lifted the baby and put her to bed. Molly didn't stir. She was probably as tired as he was. She was up at dawn and off to the school. She'd taken over the care of the house. She'd been getting up at night with Lass for the past week, a relief for him since they were so busy with the cattle.

He slipped a hand behind her and one under her legs and lifted her into his arms. She weighed less than some of the calves they'd been roping and branding.

She laid her head on his shoulder and murmured against his neck. "It's late."

"I know." He carried her down the hall. Pushing the door closed behind him with his shoulder, he hesitated. The moonlight threw a square of light on the covers, all turned back and ready.

If he laid her there, would she notice?

Without giving himse! time to answer the question, he walked to the bed and laid her on it. She sighed without opening her eyes. He reached down to pull the covers over her. Instead he touched her hair and smoothed it on the pillow.

"Molly," he said.

She opened her eyes.

The moonlight cast the room into silver-edged shadows. It created a halo of light around Sam as he bent toward her. It made the night magic.

Slowly, so very slowly, he moved beside her. She felt his weight on the mattress, then the contact of his thigh against hers. In the stillness that followed, she heard the beat of her heart, loud and insistent in her ears.

"Molly," he said, a husky whisper in the dark.

She heard the longing in him. An answering need suffused her whole body. He hadn't said the words, but she didn't think they were necessary. She knew his heart.

With a sureness borne of love, she touched him, letting her fingers meander over his chest. Her senses heightened, she was acutely aware of the crisp feel of his body hair and the warmth of his skin.

The world condensed into this moment, this place.

"Is the time right?" he murmured, his lips only a few inches from hers.

"Yes."

His chest touched hers as he drew in a deep breath, then let it out slowly. A current of sensation flowed into her breasts. Her nipples contracted almost painfully.

He placed his left hand on the bed beside her and shifted his weight to it. With his right hand, he smoothed the strands of hair from her temple, then he cupped her chin.

She held her breath as his mouth descended. Through an eternity of waiting, his lips finally touched her. It was the sweetest thing imaginable.

There was no need to think about her reactions. Her body acted on its own, knowing instinctively the right moves.

She reached for him, circling his broad shoulders with her arms, running her fingers into his hair, which was cool and damp on top, but warm in the underlayers.

His arms slipped under her, bringing her upright and deepening the kiss at the same time. He held her tightly, and she felt the *th-thump* of his heart against her, the beats fast and powerful.

Light-headed with happiness, she skimmed her hands down his back, loving the smooth ripple of muscle under his skin, exulting in his masculine strength, secure in the knowledge that he would never use it against her.

He moved his lips over hers. She opened hers, inviting him inside. He dipped lightly, the merest butterfly of a touch, again and again, then drew back to study her.

A demand pushed its way to her throat, a soft moan of need greater than the other time she'd been in his arms. She knew what to expect. She knew what she wanted. And she wanted it now, this moment.

"Easy," he murmured when she stirred restlessly in his arms.

"I want you," she confessed.

"You'll have me," he promised, a heated avowal that stirred new longing in her. He laid her against the pillow.

She'd never felt so wild, so abandoned to her senses, so very, very right in her instincts. This was her man, her mate, and she was his. This was right.

"Sam," she whispered on a shaky breath as he kissed along her neck. At the neckline to her satin pajamas, he paused.

"May I?" he asked, his fingers on the top button.

"Yes." She hardly recognized her own voice, it was so choked with love and the passion he invoked in her.

He flicked the buttons open . . . one, then another . . . another . . . and the last one. Pausing, he looked into her eyes, his handsome face serious and filled with purpose.

Sam ran his fingers inside the edge of the material and slowly pushed it to each side.

A tremor glided through him, as if his world had tilted on its axis. Molly looked up at him with complete trust in her eyes. She waited for him to complete the task he'd begun. He wasn't sure if he could go slow for her.

The moment was breathtakingly beautiful. He didn't want it to end. But the rush of anticipation burned in his blood, and he couldn't ignore the need to see her, to touch her, any longer.

Sliding the material completely off her breasts, he gazed at her, feeling like a starving man at a feast. "You're beautiful," he said, the words inadequate, but he couldn't think of any others to express how he felt.

She laid a hand in the center of his chest. "We both are. We're beautiful together."

It made perfect sense to him.

Like him, she understood, even without words, the beauty of the moment. A need to cherish her, to softly and reverently kiss every inch of her, stole over him.

The words came of their own volition. "Ah, Molly," he said, fighting for control. "Molly, darling."

He needed to be inside, buried in her warmth, in the sweet, welcoming center of her. He needed . . . her.

Moving carefully so as not to frighten her with the lust that raged through him, he slipped his thumbs under the elastic waistband of her pajamas. "Lift your hips."

She did as he wished.

With one liquid motion, he peeled the material from her. His breath caught in his throat. She lay still under the siege of his gaze and permitted him to look his fill.

"Beautiful." It was the only word he could find.

He leaned over her, letting his body skim hers ever so lightly. Her breasts beaded again, drawing into tiny buds of passion he had to taste.

Molly couldn't seem to get enough air. She gasped when his lips opened and gently sucked one nipple into his mouth. With his tongue, he teased and stroked until she writhed against him in increasing demand, wanting more . . . more . . .

"Come to me." She panted with need. "Now. Please, now." She wasn't sure what she wanted, only that he held the key.

"Not yet. I wouldn't last a second. One stroke and . . ." He smiled down at her, then nuzzled her nose with his. "I want to make love to you for hours."

"I don't think I can last that long."

His chest moved against hers as he chuckled. "I'll make sure you do." He paused. "Molly, I want to lie beside you."

She ran her hands over his back, urging him closer. "Oh, yes, please do."

He stood. With one swift movement, he stripped out of his briefs. The moonlight from the window outlined his powerful body. She vaguely wondered if she should be alarmed, but oddly, she wasn't. Her faith in her husband was absolute. He would know what to do.

With the same care as before, he lifted her and slipped the satin top off her shoulders and down her arms. It pooled on the floor with the other items of clothing.

She shivered.

He must have felt it. "Don't be afraid."

"I'm not. I'm just... anxious."

His smile flashed briefly, then his mouth was on hers again. She felt his chest, the brush of his thigh as he changed position on the bed, then... then the sheer wonder of his flesh all along hers, a hot, powerful presence that registered in every cell in her body.

For a second she was unsure about what to do next. Nature took over. She moved against him. The thrust of his body on her thigh both shocked and thrilled her.

His tongue stroked hers, coaxing her into joining his sensual play. She responded joyfully, filled with the most wonderful sensations, pressing and retreating, loving the pressure of his lips on hers.

With a knee, he nudged her legs apart. Without breaking the kiss, he moved over her, his body fitting into the grooves and angles of hers as if they'd been designed for each other.

She sucked in a quick breath when he touched the most intimate part of her. Still maintaining the kiss, he thrust gently at the jointure of her legs.

Sam didn't try to penetrate the tight closure of her body. First he wanted to get her used to his touch and to assure her he was in control. He was . . . barely.

He ignored the fierce need to thrust inside and find the peace that only she could give him. He wanted to make this first time a time to remember for her. He wanted to give her so much pleasure she'd never regret coming to him or giving him this gift of herself.

Between him and Molly, there was respect as well as passion. He could never tell her how much it meant to him. He wanted to shower her with the most exquisite pleasure she'd ever known.

That would be his gift to her for her trust.

He stroked gently at the portals of her womanhood. He kissed her breasts. A deep sense of satisfaction raced through him when she lifted to his touch, clearly indicating her desire for more.

"Yes," he encouraged. "Show me what you want."

Molly hardly heard the words. She was whirling in the haze of desire he stirred in her. It was like that night at her cottage, but better.

She loved the feel of his body on hers and was momentarily dismayed when he pulled away. But only for a second. The next instant, his mouth was on her breasts again, first one, then the other, suckling, kissing them with the heated passion they shared.

With trembling hands, she stroked through his hair and down his back. She found the small protrusions of his nipples in his chest hair and toyed with them. She glided down his torso to his abdomen. He sucked in a harsh breath when she touched him more intimately. She hesitated, then closed her hand around him.

He lifted his head and gazed at her. Motionless, they watched each other.

"We'll take this as far as you want to go," he told her. "I can stop at anytime. You only have to say the word."

She nodded. Yes, she'd known all that without him saying it. She smiled at him, deliriously happy. "If you stop, I'll bite you," she promised and pulled his chest hair with her teeth to show him.

Sam laughed and gave her a bear hug, then turned them over so she was on top. "Okay, you can explore now."

Her eyes opened wide, then narrowed as she studied him, taking her time in deciding where she wanted to go first. He gritted his teeth, determined to wait out the exquisite torture.

Curiosity got the better of her. Shifting to one side, she stroked down his stomach until she reached the destination she'd chosen.

He held his breath as she touched him, gingerly at first, with uncertain glances at his face to see how he was reacting. He remained still, a smile kicking up the corners of his mouth as she became bolder.

Hooking his hands under the headboard, he reveled in her earnest exploration. Mixed with the passion she aroused was that odd tenderness she induced. He'd never felt exactly this way about a woman before.

The moment came when she grew too bold for his self-control. Bending down, she kissed the tip of his shaft, then drew back and looked at him, her eyes dancing with seductive mischief.

He uttered an expletive as heat exploded inside him like a rocket. Turning with her in his arms, he slid between her legs and pressed the full length of his body on hers. He began to move in a smooth cadence, rubbing intimately until she moved with each motion of his.

The moonlight had shifted, and he couldn't see her face as clearly. He didn't need to. Her panting gasps and soft moans told him she was as caught in desire's net as he was.

He could feel the moisture where they met, the sweet dew of passion a woman couldn't hide. The need to take her all the way swept over him in a tidal wave of possessive tenderness.

Moving his hand between them, he stroked gently, intimately, urgently. She hesitated, but he wouldn't give her time to think about this new strategy. He kissed her mouth until they were breathless, then he kissed her some more.

Suddenly she went totally still beneath him. He gritted his teeth together and kept up the same rhythmic movements.

When she stopped breathing, he moved faster, feeling his own control slip as he sensed the coming climax.

"Sam," she whispered. "Oh...yes...oh...yes. Oh, Sam...oh, darling...oh...*yes.*"

His own breathing grew more and more ragged while she clutched his shoulders and murmured his name in a passionate delirium. He brought her down gently.

Molly couldn't lift a finger. Her bones had dissolved, and her body floated in a warm, sloshing liquid that rose and fell in gentle waves with each breath.

Sam kissed her closed eyes, then moved away.

"Don't go," she managed to murmur.

"I'm not going far."

She heard the rasp of a drawer. Opening her eyes, she saw him remove a packet from the bedside table.

"You're not on birth control, are you?" he asked, sitting up beside her.

"No." She frowned. "Sam, I'd like a baby."

He paused. "Now?" He sounded hoarse.

She wished she could see his face better. The moon had disappeared behind a hill, and the room was darker than when they'd started. "Soon. It would be nice to have a brother or sister for Lass." She sounded defensive, but couldn't help it.

"Would you mind waiting awhile?" he asked, almost formally.

"No, of course not. I didn't mean we had to start tonight, but in a few months. It's important to me."

He finished his task and returned to her. Lying beside her, he stroked her body, fondling each part as if she were the most precious thing in his world. He made her feel special.

"Is it?" he asked, more as if he were talking to himself than her, as if he were checking the idea from all angles.

"Yes. I love children. That's the one thing I wanted and thought I could never have. And now...well, it would round out our family."

"Our family," he repeated, his tone low and hoarse again. He peered into her face intently. "You mean it, don't you? You really mean it."

"Of course." She couldn't figure out why he found that a thing to marvel at. It seemed natural to want children.

"Molly," he said.

That was all, but she heard more. For some reason, her desire for children had touched him. She reached for him and pulled his mouth to hers, telling him without words how she felt.

This time when he moved between her thighs, she knew they could find completion together. He touched her as he had before, with feather strokes over her breasts and abdomen, her thighs and finally that very sensitive place that welcomed him so greedily.

She opened to him, taking him inside. They both trembled when the complete journey was made, then he lay still over her for a moment before he began the journey all over again.

Once, when she cried out and clung to him, she thought she heard him laugh, but she wasn't sure. The roar of the blood through her ears was like a gale in the cottonwoods. She was caught up, swept away, overjoyed by it.

"I love you," she told him. "I love you, love you, love you." Over and over again. Those were the only words that came close to describing the magic.

Chapter Ten

Molly watched the dawn creep across the eastern sky in tendrils of color. She lay beside her husband, happiness a core of bubbling warmth inside her. Sam slept with one arm over her waist, his face pressed into her hair.

It was nearly time for her to be up and about. The play was on for that afternoon. There was a ton of work to be done before then. Ah, but she didn't want to move. If she could stay there forever, just like that, she'd be content.

Resting her hand on his arm, she relived the moments of the night. The sense of being one with him lingered like a melody in her mind—one body, one soul, one love.

A touch on her neck followed by the coolness of moisture told her that her husband was awake.

"You taste good," he murmured, drawing a moist line up to her earlobe. He nibbled there, sending little currents of electricity down into her chest.

"It's easier," she said.

"Is that the answer?"

"Yes."

"What's the question?"

"After the night at the cottage, I wondered if it would have been easier to face you the next morning if we'd slept together that night. It would have."

He raised his head and propped up on an elbow. He peered into her face, then smiled when she held his gaze. Odd, she didn't feel embarrassed at all after sharing the most intimate of experiences with him, yet she'd dreaded her next encounter with him after that night in the kitchen.

"We're married now. We can cohabitate all we want to with everyone's blessings."

His teasing reminder of their wedding night did bring a flush to her cheeks. He laughed, then nuzzled her ear again.

"I thought you didn't want me," she said, defending herself.

"I can't believe you thought that after that first session. I nearly lost it. I was envious of Lass getting to spend the night at your house, and I couldn't."

She stroked his face and found his beard rasped against her finger when she rubbed upward. "But you could have. That was why I was embarrassed. I did lose it."

He moved suddenly, swinging his long, lean body over hers. After making love, he'd put her pajama top back on to keep her from getting cold, but the bottoms were still on the floor. From the waist down, flesh touched flesh.

She felt the nudge of his body against her. A pleasurable flash of anticipation shot through her. "Do we have time?" she asked, uncertain. It seemed they'd made love for hours during the night.

"Yes," he said. "If we concentrate."

She discovered that things could move very quickly when one concentrated. Later, she made another discovery—that showering together could be fun.

"I love you," she said, laughing helplessly as he dried her off, but mostly rubbed the places he liked best.

He stilled for a moment, then dropped the towel over her head and rubbed her hair. She wished he could say the words.

Not that it mattered. Whatever his past had been, the future was theirs to shape together. She'd work with him to see that it was as wonderful as it could be.

And he was going to have to get used to her loving him. She intended to tell him often.

A half hour later, she was ready to leave the house. Sam followed her out to the car, Lass in his arms. When the child was strapped into her seat, he paused by her door.

"Take care." His eyes caressed her, giving the words extra meaning.

"You, too." She lifted her face.

He bent down until he could kiss her.

"I love you," she murmured when he straightened. "See you at one. Don't be late." She gave him a stern glance.

Waving, she drove off. Halfway to town, she remembered what she'd been going to tell him last night.

She'd call him when she arrived in town. He might still be at the house.

No one answered the phone. On the tenth ring, Molly hung up and started to work.

"Why are you crying, Krissie?" Molly lifted the four-year-old onto her lap and wiped the tears with a tissue.

"Zack said I sounded funny," the girl said. "He said my song was *stoopid.*"

"Why did you believe him? Didn't Miss Tiffany and I say your song was very nice?"

"Y-yes," Krissie said with a snuffle. Her blue eyes were filled with doubts.

"We're your teachers. We know how the song is supposed to sound. You sing it perfectly. I would have said if you'd gotten it wrong. Your mother and grandmother are going to be very proud when they hear it."

"You think so? My brother said it was a silly song."

"Well, he is simply wrong. I wouldn't have a silly song in our play. It's a *fun* song, and our guests will like it."

"Oh."

"Let's dry those tears. We don't want you to have red eyes instead of blue ones when the parents arrive, do we?"

Molly gave Krissie an ice cube wrapped in a paper towel to hold to her eyes for a few minutes, then went to solve the next crisis. Blowing a strand of hair out of her face, she separated two trees who were fighting over their position at the front of the stage. "You stand here on the blue X, Zack. Tony goes on the red one." She gave them a stern look, which settled them down for about a tenth of a second.

Plopping into her chair, she wondered why she'd thought it would be a good idea to put on a play. The whole production was falling apart right before her eyes.

With one eye on the kids and one on the clock, she ate a square of lasagna, some vegetable sticks wrapped in a cabbage leaf and gulped down a glass of tea.

"I'm going to hang Sam from the church bell tower if he doesn't get here within the next five minutes," she muttered to Tiffany as they helped the children clean up their lunch trays.

"Did he get the house done?"

"Yes. It's adorable. I can't imagine why he's late."

"Well, he was late a lot in picking up Lass."

"Yes, but that was before..." She trailed off, thinking of her marriage and that morning and the night before. She felt married now, a part of him as he was a part of her.

"You're blushing," Tiffany said pointedly, her grin an equal mixture of envy and irony. "Marriage seems to agree with you. One month and you're blossoming. Or are you increasing, as my grandmother used to say?"

Molly fixed a stern eye on her friend. "That's between my husband and me."

Tiffany smothered a giggle. "We'll soon know. All the old biddies at church have been trying to decide if you and Sam had to get married."

"Honestly," Molly mumbled, irritated that her life and her affairs were on the tongues of the local gossips.

She heard the sound of an engine. Rushing to the window, she saw the ranch truck park and the two hands climb down. "Here they are," she called to Tiffany and went out to help.

"Where's Sam?" she asked, going behind the truck.

"Uh, something came up that he had to take care of. He'll probably be by later," Tom told her.

She ignored the disappointment and directed the men in getting the gingerbread house inside and set up for the play.

"Thirty minutes," she reminded everyone as they scurried into costumes. She pulled the sheets, which were strung on wires, across the room to hide the riser that formed the stage.

Tiffany ran to the store for ice to go in the punch that would be served during the social hour after the play. The first parents and neighbors arrived. Molly supervised her "greeters" at the door. The guests were escorted to their seats.

Finally it was time. The folding chairs, borrowed from the church, were filled. Sandy and Tom stayed for the drama. She wished Sam could have come and wondered what he was doing that was so important.

Just as she and Tiffany were about to pull the curtains, the door opened again, blowing the sheets inward. She peeked out and saw Elsie Tisdale slip inside. Molly smiled at the woman. When she had time, she'd find out what had happened to Sam.

"Ready?" Tiffany whispered loudly. There was a titter of laughter from the guests.

Molly nodded. The play was on.

An hour later, they closed the sheets on a happy family reunion as the father of the children held their hands and they all danced around in a circle while the trees and bluebirds of the enchanted forest sang the closing song. Krissie's voice soared above the others in a sweet, true treble.

The applause was tremendous.

"Wonderful, children," she told them. "That was a very successful play. I am so proud of us all."

She had to help the children out of their costumes before she could find out about Sam. She hoped the men didn't leave before she could get to them. She'd told them to stay for cookies and punch, then they could take the gingerbread house back to the ranch.

She had a feeling there was trouble. What it could be, she had no idea. A heaviness settled in her stomach.

At last, the sheets were pulled back for the last time, and the actors mingled with the guests.

Molly went to the kitchen alcove to check on Lass, who'd shown how she felt about the play by sleeping right through it.

The baby was gone.

Startled, she glanced around, but didn't see the child with Tiffany or anyone. She looked under the crib just to be sure Lass hadn't slipped out of the bed, landed on the floor and rolled out of sight. Panic began to flutter through her, making it hard to breathe.

"Elsie," she said and whirled around.

The woman wasn't in the room. Molly, smiling at parents and trying to appear calm, hurried to the door and out onto the sidewalk. She went limp with relief.

Elsie and Lass were in the Tisdale ranch vehicle. A sharp rebuke sprang to Molly's lips, but when she stopped by the car, it died. The older woman had tears running down her face.

"Elsie, what is it?"

Elsie wiped her eyes and turned to Molly. Lass, sitting in her grandmother's lap, was exploring a new toy.

Molly knelt by the open car door, perplexed and concerned by Mrs. Tisdale's ravaged face.

"I was supposed to steal her," she said.

Molly jerked in shock. "Why? You couldn't possibly get away with it. That would be kidnapping."

"William thought it would prove you weren't good parents. He thought we could show the judge you didn't keep a watch on Lass, that anybody could have taken her."

"Why didn't you leave?" Molly asked gently.

Elsie shook her head. "I couldn't." Her lips trembled. "Lass is a happy baby. You and Sam have made a good home for her. I couldn't snatch her away from a happy home and bring her to ours."

Molly shoved her hair back from her face. "Why does he hate Sam? It's like an obsession."

"Sam's a success. That's reason enough." Her eyes beseeched Molly to understand. "Once William was handsome. He had money and looks and a fast car. All the girls were crazy about him. His father died when he was little, and his mother spoiled him. So did I. We thought, his mother and I, that the sun rose and set with him. But money... none of us knew how to make it, only spend it. Now we're about to lose everything."

"And William is too proud to ask Sam for help," Molly concluded.

"Yes. He asked Sam to join operations, but Sam wouldn't." She hesitated. "Sam said Lass's money was in an irrevocable trust."

"It is. Sam has made me the trustee in case of his death. Did William think he would get the use of the money if Lass were put in his custody?"

"I think so. We stopped telling each other our plans and dreams long ago." She sighed. "I no longer have any, and I don't care about his."

"Oh, but you must," Molly protested. "It's most often the woman who carries the dreams for the whole family, who sees everyone's potential and encourages them. If the mother gives up, the entire family can be lost."

Elsie looked at her as if she were speaking a foreign language. Molly stopped her sermonizing. "You didn't take Lass away," she said softly. "That proves you care about something. Lass loves you, too. She watches for you each day."

"Don't spoil her the way William and I did with Elise. She was a terror—defiant and rude and self-centered." She handed the child to Molly. "But you won't ruin Lass. I can see that already. Your love is the good kind."

Lass patted Molly's cheek, then leaned forward to give her a sloppy kiss. Molly's heart squeezed into a tight knot. That often happened around Lass and Sam. She had so much love she felt her body wasn't big enough to hold all of it.

"All love is good, but it has to be tempered with discipline and the expectation of good manners. Speaking of which, I need to find out what happened to Sam. He was supposed to be here for the play. He made the gingerbread house."

"It was lovely. Everything was. The little girl who sang was very good. She reminded me of Elise at that age."

Molly stood and laid a hand on Elsie's shoulder. "Will you come back?"

Their eyes met in wordless questions and answers. Elsie nodded. "Nothing can keep me away. You don't have to worry. I won't do anything to hurt Lass."

"I know that. That's why I trust you."

Pleased surprise appeared on Elsie's face. "Do you? Even though I tried to leave with her?"

"You didn't. That's what counts. Do come back. Lass needs you. Her grandfather, too."

Elsie shook her head. "I don't think anyone can reach William now. He's let things go too far—" She broke off.

Uneasiness traveled the bumpy road of Molly's spine. "What has he done?"

"Nothing. So far. I'll talk to him." Her lips firmed with purpose, and she looked younger, almost prettier as she sat up straight and started the car.

"Wave bye-bye, Lass," Molly encouraged. "Wave bye-bye to Nana." She watched Elsie leave with a sense of foreboding. Then she headed back inside to find out what had delayed Sam.

Probably a cow with the sniffles. He practically hand-raised the whole herd. It was one of the best outfits in those parts according to the cowhands. She'd been so proud of Sam when they'd told her. She headed back inside.

Molly parked at the sheriff's office. It was the first time she'd had an occasion to go there in the ten years she'd lived in the area. A frown, perplexed and concerned, etched itself on her forehead. The men said a deputy sheriff had come out to the ranch. He'd asked Sam to come in to town for questioning.

Questioning for what?

It sounded ominous, like something out of one of those police shows on television.

Inside she asked for Deputy Merritt and was directed to a room down a long corridor painted institutional green. She instantly disliked the place.

She knocked at the door. A burly command to "Come in" made her tense even more. Inside her gaze flew to Sam, sitting in a straight-back chair, his face giving nothing away.

"Molly," he said in surprise. He was displeased.

She went to him, dropping into a squat to study him and make sure he hadn't been hurt. "Are you all right?"

His grin, tough and cynical, kicked up the corners of his mouth. "Sure. They haven't got out the rubber hoses yet." He smoothed her hair from her temple. "I told the guys not to tell you."

"They had to. I was threatening to turn the kids loose on them." She tried a smile, and found she could hold it.

"That would convince them."

"Excuse me?"

Molly looked around.

"You Ms. Frazier?"

"Yes. Molly Frazier. Why are you holding my husband? Has he been charged with anything?"

"It hasn't got to that."

"He's been here for over an hour," she reminded the officer. She knew something about the law from helping her brother study when they were both college students. "Did they read you your rights?" she asked Sam.

"No."

She turned on the deputy, ready to read him the riot act. Sam clasped her hand and tugged on it. "Sit down and relax, Molly. They just wanted to ask a few questions."

"They can't charge you with anything without reading the Miranda Act rights to you, and they can't hold you indefinitely without telling you your crime."

"Thanks," Sam said dryly. "When I need a defense attorney, I'll call you."

She didn't think Sam was taking this with the seriousness it deserved. She knew how people's minds worked. No matter how innocent Sam was—and she knew he hadn't done anything wrong—there were those who thought, because he'd been picked up for questioning, that he must be guilty of something. The old *where there's smoke, there's fire* syndrome.

"Could I see you outside?" the deputy asked.

Her eyes darted to Sam, a question in them. He shrugged, his face as blank as a stone wall.

Facing the deputy detective, she shook her head. "You can ask me whatever you like, but in front of Sam." She held out her hand. "I don't think we've met."

Sam almost laughed as the deputy and Molly shook hands and exchanged greetings as if they were at a damn tea party.

"Bill Merritt, Ms. Frazier. My niece was in your school before she started kindergarten this year. My sister says you helped Dottie a lot. She used to be sort of difficult."

"Oh, Dottie," Molly exclaimed affectionately. "She's a lovely child. She needed a bit of help in learning to finish her tasks and perhaps a few social skills. I'm sure she's going to be a fine student. She was very bright."

Sam felt the familiar tenderness swell like a spring blossom waiting to burst forth. No wonder her students loved her. Molly looked on the bright side and saw the good in everyone.

Uneasiness washed over him. He hoped she kept faith with him after this episode with the law. Anger burned in him at the turn of events that afternoon. He'd been hauled down to the county sheriff's office for questioning about a rustling incident.

Legally he had no "priors." His youthful escapade, done to prevent his stepfather from stealing and selling off any more of the ranch's cattle, had backfired. He'd been arrested for rustling when he tried to hide a small herd.

The charges had been dropped, but no one had believed in his motives or innocence, not even his own mother. As a man, he'd forgiven her for that, but it had been hard.

He glanced at Molly and away. Would she believe in him? He steeled himself for the opposite, for the disappointment that would darken her eyes to stormy gray when she realized the charges being investigated.

"What's happened?" Molly asked the deputy in a quiet tone. Her manner implied that she understood there was a problem and she was equipped to handle it. The schoolmarm in control.

Bill shifted uncomfortably. "There was some trouble last night. A man got shot—he's going to be fine," he added quickly at her expression of concern. "It was out near your place, on a spread east of the Pecos. A rancher found his fence had been cut out by the county road. Some cattle were missing. He followed the tracks of a truck and found one man standing guard with the herd. Instead of going home and calling in the law, he decided to play hero and arrest the man. Got himself shot in the shoulder."

"That's terrible." Molly looked from the officer to Sam and back. "But I don't understand. What has Sam to do with this?"

"Well, uh, he was involved in a rustling operation once before, so I had to bring him in for questioning."

"Questioning for what?"

"For the rustling."

Sam knew the minute Molly realized that *he* was being questioned as the culprit. Her eyes flew open, then narrowed into spear points. She crossed her arms, shifted her weight to one hip and thrust the other out as if she might start patting her foot any minute.

"Sam didn't do any rustling. It's ludicrous that you think he would. He runs a very successful ranch."

The deputy's ears turned a dull red. "Well, there was that other time—"

"He was sixteen years old. The charges were dropped. Even if they hadn't been, his record would have been wiped clean when he became eighteen. That's the law." She gave poor Bill her I'm-really-disappointed-in-you look.

Sam felt sorry for the man as he hemmed and hawed, trying to explain why he had to do his job. "Can you vouch for Frazier last night?" he finally asked.

"Of course I can." She was in fine form now—indignant and hot on the trail of justice. "Sam was with me last night." She looked at him. A red tide swept up her face.

Sam grew hot, too, but not from embarrassment at remembering what had happened between them. Every time he thought of last night, a fiery arrow shot straight through him, lodging in his groin where he became hard and throbbing.

"Can you give me some idea of the time you were together?" The deputy got out his notepad.

"Yes. He came in at eleven. I know because Lass has been cranky of late. She's cutting teeth."

Molly and the officer exchanged glances of understanding and sympathy. Sam mentally shook his head at how easily she could bring a person over to her side.

She continued. "Lass and I'd gone to sleep in the rocker in her room. Sam came in and put Lass to bed and—" she lifted her chin "—and carried me to our bed and tucked me in. We were together the rest of the night and this morning until Lass and I left for school shortly after seven."

"You sure it was eleven when he came in?"

"Yes. I heard the kitchen clock strike the hour and looked at the clock on Lass's wall. It was eleven."

"And he stayed in bed the rest of the night?"

"Yes. I'm a light sleeper. I'd have known if he got up."

"There was blood on his truck."

She nodded. "He helped birth a calf last night. That's why he was late getting in. I put his shirt and pants in cold water to soak out the bloodstains. You probably saw them if you went out to the ranch."

Sam gave the man a sardonic smile. Her story agreed with his. The rustling had taken place in the wee hours of the morning. It had been pure luck that the rancher had seen the cut wires when he came in from a late poker game.

Fortunately for Sam, there wasn't enough time for him to do the dirty deed between the time he was last seen by his two hands and the time he arrived home and found Molly asleep in the chair.

Bill asked a few more perfunctory questions, but it was clear the deputy considered Sam off the hook.

The detective hadn't believed him, but Molly's word was as good as gold in the bank. His attorney had been right about marrying her.

However, it didn't set well with Sam to hide behind a woman's skirts. His word ought to count for something.

The lawman let him go with a promise to keep them informed of future developments. Molly beamed her approval. The deputy beamed back. Sam shook his head in resignation.

Outside, he walked her to her car. "How about some lunch? I missed it during the excitement."

"Well, I should get back to school." She grinned up at him, looking for all the world like a teenager about to play hooky. "I'll keep you company while you eat." She paused and studied him before getting in the compact sedan.

He tensed and waited for the accusations to come. His mother had had the charges dropped against him, but only to protect the family name. She hadn't believed his tale of saving the ranch. He steeled himself for the suspicion that would show up in Molly's face.

He'd been an outcast before. He could take it.

Her eyes searched his, then she surprised him by throwing her arms around his shoulders and giving him a fierce hug. "Are you very angry?"

"For what?" He hesitated, then put his arms around her.

"For being questioned. Anyone who knows you should know you're not a thief. You're one of the most honorable people I've ever met. And the gentlest. With Lass and with me. Last night, you were wonderful, simply wonderful.''

A ball of emotion leapt into his chest. For a moment, he couldn't speak. His throat clogged up, and a terrible pressure built behind his eyes. All because this woman believed in him . . . really believed in him.

''You're one of a kind, Molly,'' he managed to whisper. ''One of a kind.''

And she was his. *His.*

Chapter Eleven

"You said you could ride," Sam reminded Molly at noon on Saturday. "I thought we might take a lunch and ride up the Pecos a ways. There's a pretty spot for a picnic by the river."

"I'd love it." Worry nicked a frown between her brows. "What about Lass? It's almost nap time."

"I have a carrier."

Fifteen minutes later, they set off, Lass strapped into a baby harness in front of Sam. He was mounted on a big, bony gelding that Molly had discovered was a prince of a horse, good-natured and easygoing. Her own steed, also a gelding, was smaller and quite feisty.

"Painter's got a rough gait," Sam had told her, "but he's as surefooted as they come."

She didn't know about the surefooted part, but she could vouch for the rough gait. When Painter trotted, it was like sitting astride a jackhammer going full blast.

She mentioned this fact to Sam after they galloped across a broad meadow. He merely grinned. The brute.

"Look, Sam, tire tracks," she called at one point. "Were you up here in the truck recently?"

He circled back and studied the tracks when she pointed them out. They formed a faint trail through the dust and sage.

"One of the boys might have been. I don't remember."

She took a deep breath of the sage-scented air. "I can see why you love this place. Look at the view."

He studied her instead, making her self-conscious about her windblown appearance. Although she wore a hat, freckles tended to pop out on her nose at the least hint of sun on her face.

Sam glanced at the tracks again, then clicked to his mount. Lass clicked, too, drawing a laugh from Molly. She clicked and her horse fell into step behind Sam's mount.

The day was beautiful, perfect for dancing around the Maypole as folks used to do in olden times. She could recall doing it herself in elementary school.

"Maybe next year we'll plan a Maypole Dance for the students," she said, sharing her idea.

"Do I have to build it?"

"Of course."

"It'll cost you," he warned. "Be careful along here. We have to climb a ridge."

Molly discovered the little gelding was adept at getting between a rock and a hard place. By the time they came out on a rocky ledge overlooking the river, she was holding on to the saddle horn and being careful not to look down.

Once up, she discovered they then had to go down. She gritted her teeth and stared at Sam's back until they stopped.

Sam dismounted and came to her. "At least you didn't close your eyes," he commented.

"I was too scared. I didn't want to miss something to grab hold of in case Painter went over the bluff."

Her husband laughed as he swung the saddlebags off his horse. He untied a blanket and spread it over a grassy patch of ground under the cottonwood trees. He placed Lass on it.

"You going to get down?" he asked, giving her a quizzical look.

"I can't. My legs are numb."

He shook his head and held up his arms to her. She fell into them and moaned when she tried to stand on her own. Sam looked concerned.

"I'm okay. It's just that . . . after all that riding last night, and then today . . ." The thought trailed off, and heat climbed her face. She wasn't as bold in speaking of their lovemaking as she'd thought she could be.

Understanding dawned. He touched her hair. "I should have realized you'd be—"

She placed a hand over his mouth. "Actually I was hoping you'd brought me up here to ravish me where my cries for help wouldn't be heard."

He wound the strand of hair around and around his finger, bringing her closer and closer to his mouth. "They didn't sound like cries for help last night. It sounded to me like cries for more. I seem to remember a *don't stop* in there . . . and *please* . . ." His lips were very near hers.

"Well, whatever." She shrugged nonchalantly.

Suddenly she was caught up against a broad chest, her mouth definitely ravished by his in a long kiss of leashed emotion.

When he let her go, they were both breathing hard.

"We'd better feed Lass before she realizes she hasn't had lunch yet," she suggested, shaken by the intensity of the kiss.

He'd kissed her that way last night, too, with a desperate silence that sliced right down to her soul. She wasn't sure what he felt, but whatever the emotion, it was powerful, driving him to hold and kiss her for hours, to make love until they were sated and exhausted, and still he'd held her…all night…as if he'd never let her go.

They settled on the blanket with their daughter. She laid out their sandwiches while Sam fed Lass. She poured them each a cup of lemonade from a canteen. Sipping hers, she watched her husband—in every sense of the word—as he lifted the spoon.

Her heart contracted painfully. She loved Lass as her own, but she wanted to have a baby with Sam, too. Watching him with the child, thinking of his care of the animals on the ranch, his respect for his two ranch hands, his kindness toward her, she knew this man was special, so very special.

"I love you," she said softly, compelled by the urging of her heart to say the words.

"How do you know?" he asked, giving her an odd glance as he wiped Lass's sticky fingers after finishing the jars of baby food. "Was it love or a satisfying of the senses that we shared last night?"

She ignored the hurt his question caused. "Lust?" she mused aloud. "Well, there is that. It's usually the beginning between a man and a woman, but there has to be more to form a lasting bond. I think we have that."

He was silent for a long time. "So do I."

Her gaze flew to his. He gave her an earnest smile. She searched the rich darkness of his eyes and wondered if he was telling her he loved her.

"We were friends before we were lovers," he continued softly. Lass had crawled into his lap and was snuggling down like a fawn in a bed of leaves. "That we're friends afterward seems like a miracle to me. I've never known a woman like you, one that a man can share things with."

She knew if she didn't lighten the mood, she might cry. And she didn't know why or whether they'd be happy tears or sad ones.

Because he was glad of their friendship? Because he couldn't call it love? Because they did share something special between them? She didn't know.

Adopting a teasing grin, she informed him they were going to be friends and lovers for a long time. "You can have other friends," she told him generously, "but there'd better not be any other lovers besides me. I'm quite firm on that, Sam."

"You'll never have to worry." He leaned over—carefully because of the sleeping baby—and kissed her. "You're the best lover I've ever had."

That surprised her. It must have shown on her face.

"The very best," he said with quiet sincerity.

She felt beautiful and desirable and lots of other nice things. "Thank you," she said with deliberate primness. "We aim to please."

Sam chuckled and accepted the sandwich she handed him. Together they ate and watched the play of sunlight on the river. The water, golden-hued from the silt it carried, flowed with a swift rush to the Rio Grande.

Sam rearranged Lass, then settled with his head in Molly's lap. She was aware of him watching her before his eyes drifted closed. Leaning against the cottonwood tree, she watched a hawk soar in the sky. A deer appeared on the other side of the river, drank from it and cautiously slipped away. A squirrel made sleepy noises above her.

The peace of the afternoon settled around her as if it were a comforting blanket. She, too, went to sleep.

A patrol car was parked in the shade next to the house when they returned at five.

Sam frowned, then forced himself to relax when he saw the worried glances Molly cast his way. For her sake, he'd be polite no matter what developed.

Bill Merritt stepped out of the light shade of the mesquites and returned Molly's friendly wave.

"Hello," she called. "We've been on a picnic up on the river. It was simply marvelous."

Merritt nodded and looked slightly ashamed.

Sam swung down, one hand holding Lass securely against him. "What brings you out this way?"

He helped Molly dismount, catching her discreet grimace as she swung her leg free of the saddle. A pang of regret as well as amusement coursed through him. He realized he'd have to play the gentleman and let her rest tonight. She wasn't used to being a wife.

"Problems," the deputy answered his question.

"The same ones?"

"Yeah."

Sam nodded. "Why don't you take Lass in?" he suggested to Molly. "I'll take care of the horses."

She wore a troubled look but she didn't argue. "Would you like a glass of iced tea?" she asked the deputy.

"Not now, but thanks for asking. I'll talk to Sam for a minute before I mosey along home."

She took Lass and went into the house. Sam let out a breath of relief. He had some things to discuss with Merritt.

Bill followed him into the stable, lingering by the door while he removed the saddles and brushed down the horses before giving them a pail of oats.

"More rustling?" he asked when the man didn't speak.

"Yeah, south of your place this time. Thought I would warn you. There're rumors in the county. Ranchers are arming their hands, although the sheriff warned them not to."

"You worried that I'll get shot?" The question was sardonic. "Think I should give myself up now?"

Bill pushed his hat back. "Don't be a fool, Frazier. I'm not after you, but . . . I think someone is."

Sam looked questioningly at the deputy.

"Your name is being linked with the rumors. I suppose you were with the missus last night and today?"

"Yeah, I was with Molly."

"Well, I think someone is using your place as a staging area. You got some wild country back of your ranch, easy to hide a herd on it."

"You told anybody else your suspicions?"

"Only the sheriff."

A smile crooked Sam's mouth. The sheriff was the same person who'd arrested him years ago. "Well, he was probably impressed with your deductions. How come he didn't send you out to arrest me?"

"I talked him out of it."

Sam studied the detective, who was around his age. "Because of Molly?" he asked, a tightening in his gut.

"Partly," the man admitted, meeting his gaze. "Also, I don't convict a man before I have evidence."

"But someone has." Sam thrust his hands into his back pockets and walked outside the dim stable with the deputy.

"By the way, Molly spotted some tire tracks in the pasture near Deer Ridge today. The tracks veered off toward the ravine."

"The one that drops down to the river on your side?"

"Yes. I thought I'd head over that way in the morning and see if I could find out who was sightseeing on my land."

"Don't go taking the law in your own hands," Bill advised.

"Then you'd better come with me."

"Yeah, maybe I'd better 'cause you sure as hell aren't going to listen to reason."

Sam laughed. "You can talk reason all you want on the way over there. Let's meet at that old trailhead at the south end of the ridge. Seems like a good starting place."

"Right. Nine o'clock?"

Sam gave him a pained look. "This is a ranch, not a banker's office. We start at six."

Merritt muttered an expletive, then grinned. "I'll see you there. Keep this under your hat, okay?"

"Sure. Is this an official investigation?"

Merritt gave him an irritated frown. "Yes, but it's on my own time, so don't give me any grief. Or make me regret including you in on it."

Sam nodded in reply to the steely-eyed stare he got from the lawman before Merritt strode to his patrol car and left.

He helped the men with the evening chores before going to the house and facing Molly's curiosity. He didn't want to worry her about rustling operations carried out on his... *their* place.

When they went to the kitchen for supper, he saw she had bathed and changed into pink cotton slacks and a matching knit top. Lass, clean and smiling, played in her high chair.

While the men were hanging up their hats and taking their places, Sam went over to his wife. He had a feeling he was about to make a fool of himself over her, but it didn't matter.

She glanced at him with a smile. "Could you bring that platter? Be careful. It's hot."

"Sure, but first..." He leaned over and kissed her solidly on the mouth.

She was surprised, but pleased. "What was that for?"

"Because," he said. "Just because."

"That's an excellent reason."

He found, later that night, that Molly didn't want him to be a gentleman and let her rest. She turned to him, restless with need as soon as they were alone in their room.

"Love me," she whispered. "Love me now."

"I will," he promised, his head swimming with the passion she induced in him. "Always."

Molly pushed the flying tendrils of hair back from her face. "You heard what?"

Tiffany repeated the rumor. "It's all over town. About Sam being arrested last Friday."

"He was not arrested," Molly stated flatly, but softly. The children were napping. She and Tiffany were having lunch.

Indignation welled in her, a rising pool of anger on Sam's behalf. She huffed with annoyance at how ready people were to believe the worst of another person.

"Well, he was brought in," her assistant reminded her in an apologetic tone.

"He drove in voluntarily and talked to Bill Merritt at the sheriff's office."

"Did they have any evidence?"

"No." Molly bit the word off, then was ashamed for her shortness. "The only reason they had for questioning Sam was that episode when he was a teenager."

"Oh, yes, I remember." Tiffany looked away. "People are talking about that, too."

"I can imagine—*that Frazier boy, always knew he'd turn out bad,*" she parodied the gossip going around. "They're jealous that he came back and turned the ranch around. Instead of picking up his land cheap in a bankruptcy sale, they had to watch while he made good."

She stopped when she realized the other teacher was staring at her with a curious expression.

"You really love him, don't you?" Tiffany said, not really a question, but a realization on her part.

"Of course. Why would I marry him otherwise?"

"I wasn't sure. You were both so... calm about it. I never even saw him steal a kiss when he dropped Lass off, either before or after you were engaged."

Molly took another bite of the soup she'd made when she first arrived at the nursery school. Chicken noodle was one of her favorites, but she hardly noticed what she was eating.

Sam had ridden out at first light yesterday and today. She'd spent Sunday with Lass, staying close to the house, waiting for Sam to return. It had been dark when he came in.

She recalled the grim weariness on his face when he'd returned in the truck and the horse trailer with two horses in it that he pulled behind the truck. She'd held Lass and watched while he groomed and fed the animals.

"Who was with you?" she'd asked.

"Merritt."

"What were you looking for?"

"Whatever we found."

"Did you find anything?"

"No."

This morning he'd done the same, leaving with two horses in the trailer, heading for parts unknown. She hadn't said anything to him about being careful. She'd simply put her arms around his waist and snuggled against him. He'd let her hold him for a minute, then he'd gently moved her aside and left.

Molly sighed. They hadn't made love last night.

Tiffany touched her arm. "Don't worry. I'm sure it's going to be all right."

It wasn't.

As the month crept by, as the mesa bloomed and hummed with life, the situation grew worse. The parents of Molly's students wouldn't meet her eyes when they left their children or picked them up. If they did, she saw sympathy or pity in their gazes before they glanced away. The locals thought Sam was guilty.

On Friday night, she was ready when Sam came in. She followed him from the kitchen, where he left his boots, to their bedroom. Dust boiled off him like vapor with every step. He looked as if he'd been riding drag on a monthlong cattle drive and had just hit town. He headed for the shower.

When he returned to the bedroom, Molly had clean jeans, briefs and a white shirt laid out on the bed. She couldn't help watching as he finished towel-drying his hair. She liked him best as he was, without a stitch on his hard, lean frame.

The desire to caress him all over almost overpowered her earlier decision. She forced it into abeyance.

"Get dressed," she said. "We're going to town."

He tossed the towel over the back of a chair and gave her a look she couldn't decipher...sort of belligerent. He'd never given her a cross glance before. It briefly unnerved her.

"What for?"

"I want to go dancing. Tom will watch Lass," she said to waylay any protests. "I thought we'd have dinner at the truck stop, too. It's been a while since we were there."

"No."

"Yes."

"Dammit, Molly—"

"Yes," she reiterated. She gave him glare for glare, determined to have her way in this one thing. She hadn't said a word all week about him searching for the thieves all alone.

"Why?" he finally asked after a tense silence.

"Because I want to."

He frowned at her. A smile popped on her face. He eyed it suspiciously, but he was wavering.

She removed the slippers she wore at home and put on a sexy pair of sling-back high-heel evening shoes. After refreshing her lipstick, she ran a brush through her hair.

He watched her the whole time, although he'd managed to pull on the briefs during the interval. She finished and turned to face him.

"I want you to do this for me," she said, putting it quite simply. Her body stopped functioning while she waited.

He nodded and picked up the jeans.

Molly let out a relieved sigh. She didn't have a backup plan in case he'd refused. "I'll check on Lass." She hurried down the hall. Lass was asleep.

She closed the door and went to the kitchen. There, she rang Tom on the intercom and told him they were ready to leave.

Sam joined her, his face grim. She lifted her chin. No one would hurt Sam while she was present. No one.

The first person Sam saw when they entered the truck stop was the minister and his wife. "There's Mr. and Mrs. Liscomb," Molly said pointedly and waved at them across the crowded room. "Let's say hello."

The reason for the trip came to him. His wife—his do-gooder, determined-to-do-her-part-for-him wife— was showing the world what a jewel he was. Molly took his hand and tugged him along in her wake. She tossed out greetings left and right.

He muttered a curse.

She gave him her behave-yourself look.

For his own part, he didn't give a damn what the rest of the world thought of him. But he did care what Molly thought.

They stopped by the preacher's table. "Hello," Molly said cheerfully. She chatted about the weather they'd been having recently and declared spring in New Mexico was the most beautiful time and place in the world. "Don't you agree, Sam?" she asked, forcing him into the farce of friendliness.

Mrs. Liscomb eyed him with the same interest she'd give a scorpion who climbed in her lap. Molly looked at him, her heart in her eyes. He swallowed. There was no way in hell he could disappoint Molly. She was just so damn *kindhearted*. To hurt her...well, a man had to live with himself and his conscience.

"Yes, darling, I do," he dutifully responded.

Her eyes widened at the endearment, then she beamed at him as if he'd given her a wonderful gift. Her hand squeezed his.

He wished they were home so he could make love to her. Only when he was lost in her magic did he forget the world and that it thought he was a thief and a liar. Only with Molly did he find ease from a pain deep inside at a place he hadn't realized contained a sore spot. Only since she'd married him, or maybe since she'd told him of her love did he look forward to a future for them. Only with Molly.

He didn't know whether she loved him or not. He was no longer sure what love was. But if it was loyalty, she loved him. If it was faith, she loved him. If it was everything true and good, then she loved him. Because she'd given him all those.

"I'm glad the rain slacked off," he continued casually. "I've been riding the back ridges, looking for clues to the thieving that's been going on for the past month or so and keeping an eye on my herd."

A bubble of silence surrounded them at his words. He glanced around, meeting the eyes of neighboring ranchers, letting them know he knew the gossip about him and that his place hadn't been hit because he was taking care it didn't.

"There's Tiffany and Bill," Molly said. "We're joining them." She wished the reverend and his lady a good evening and pulled Sam over to another table, where she took a seat. "Well, this is nice," she remarked.

"Right," he said sardonically. He arched an eyebrow at the deputy, who smiled widely.

The man had been in on the conspiracy to get him into town and have him seen with friends whose reputations were as solid as a brass door knocker. Instead of making him rebellious as it once might have, the experience gave him that tight, squeezed feeling inside he often got around Molly and Lass.

He'd been a loner for years. For a few months, six in all, there'd been a sexual, mindless joy in his first marriage. That hadn't lasted long. With Molly, he'd found the true pleasure of friendship. It was nice. Real nice.

Even Tiffany had come over to his side. She smiled and chatted without one wary glance his way. He wondered how much the deputy had to do with her change of heart.

Love. It was in the air.

He was intensely aware of Molly beside him. She looked especially pretty tonight in a pair of black slacks and a black-and-gold top. The black high heels were so damn sexy he wanted to kiss her toes...and work up from there.

"Right, darling?" she asked.

"Uh, right."

The other three laughed.

He grinned. "What was the question?"

"I asked if dancing wasn't your favorite pastime."

Hardly. His favorite pastime was making love to his wife. "As long as it isn't more complicated than the two-step."

"I don't know how to do the two-step," she admitted.

"I'll teach you."

She smiled with delight at her husband. With Molly, no task was impossible. Look at the headway she was making with the mustang. He would stand for hours while she brushed him, which she liked to do. She was spoiling the horse.

After the meal, the four of them went to a night spot that featured Western music. Sam ordered a pitcher of margaritas.

"I'll go to sleep," Molly warned, lifting her glass for the first sip.

Sam leaned close. "Not for long," he promised.

She laughed and tried a sultry glance from under her lashes.

"Keep that up and we'll go home now." He took her hand and swung up from his chair. "There's our song."

He showed her how to do the basics of the Texas Two-step. After she had that down, he taught her several variations. By the third dance, she was trying out her own steps.

"Hey, wait for me," he called, catching up when she spun off on her own. He caught her in his arms.

She wrapped her arms around his neck and danced in close, her body plastered all along his. She sighed happily. "I love dancing," she told him.

"It has its moments." His voice was husky as he tightened his arms around her.

Leaning back, she gazed into his eyes. She shook her head so her hair fell back behind her shoulders and swung out when he spun them around. "I feel incredibly sexy."

His chest lifted against hers. "You are, darling."

"You called me that earlier. At the restaurant. It was the first time—"

"Not the first." He corrected her.

"I meant, in front of other people, not just when we're making love."

"Shh," he cautioned, but he was smiling. "Okay, here we go." He twirled her around, then into a dip as the song ended.

Molly laughed happily. The night was magic. She was soaring. She could touch the moon...but touching her husband was so much nicer. She nibbled on his ear when she had the chance.

"Stop that, or we'll have to go home now."

By midnight, she'd learned the Electric Slide plus two other line dances. "You're really good," Tiffany said. "It took me ages to remember the steps."

"After all the reels and folk dances we've taught at school, these are a snap."

"It took me ages to remember those, too," Tiffany complained with a mock sigh. "Fortunately we rehearsed a lot."

Molly sipped her margarita. She looked at her glass in surprise. It was full. "Is this glass magic? I was sure I'd drunk half of it."

"The waiter refills them when he comes by. Don't worry. I'm keeping an eye on you," Sam said with a lazy grin.

She gazed at him solemnly. "I'll try not to embarrass you."

"You couldn't." He met her gaze.

She became lost in the compelling depths of his eyes while love consumed her in its gentle flames. She'd be glad when they were alone so she could touch him completely. Thinking of his hands on her, stroking and coaxing her to greater heights of bliss, her breath caught in a rapturous sigh.

"Come on, let's dance," Bill invited Tiffany. "These two need to be alone."

Molly straightened. A blush climbed her face.

Sam touched her cheek. "I like it when you look at me that way," he murmured for her ears alone. "As if I'm the only man in the world you see."

"You are."

He swallowed hard. "I know. Come on. One more dance, and then we'll mosey along."

When she came into his arms, so sweetly willing, he fought a losing battle with his conscience. He no longer cared if it was lust that drew her to him. Whatever they shared, it was good, and that was all that mattered.

Tenderness stole over him. It reached right down to that sore place in his soul, pressing hard so that it was both painful and satisfying. He couldn't explain the sensation, only knew that it was there and it was because of the woman in his arms.

His wife.

"One more song," he murmured before they sat down. "Wait."

Molly watched him go to the band leader. Money exchanged hands. Sam had requested a song. She smiled dreamily when he came back to her. They were the only couple on the floor.

When the music started, Sam reached for her. They danced, alone on the floor, alone in the world as far as she was concerned. Tears filled her eyes as love filled her heart.

"Do you love me, Molly darlin'? Let your answer be a kiss," Sam sang softly to her.

Cupping his face in her hands, she kissed him.

Whistles and thunderous clapping brought her out of her daze. She looked around the dim room. Everyone was laughing and applauding them. She smiled and blew kisses.

"Come on, dream girl. It's time to go home."

Chapter Twelve

"Easy, boy," Sam said to the gelding.

The big horse flicked one ear toward Sam. He shook his head, showing his impatience at being reined in.

Sam pulled firmly, stopping the horse under the shadows of a juniper where it would be harder to spot them, in case anyone was looking. Lifting binoculars, he searched the area thoroughly.

Nothing.

But something had the big gelding excited. Could be a herd of wild horses, of course. Or maybe there was someone else on his land, such as cattle thieves. They would have to be on horses in this country. It was too rough for vehicles.

He rode on after a spell of sitting and watching. Ahead of him was the big arroyo. It was a quarter-mile long, dropping down to the river from the mesa.

During hard storms, water rushed along its rocky seams so fast it could kill a man. One of the wild horses that roamed the area had been found in the bottom last year. It had drowned.

He checked the sky. Not a cloud in sight.

Some cautionary instinct caused him to dismount before he showed himself at the rim. There, back-lighted by the sky, he'd be an easy target, if someone was in the mood for practice.

After tying his mount to a young mesquite, he walked to the edge of the dry wash, keeping a heap of boulders between him and the rim. Climbing over and between the rocks, keeping his head low, he eased out onto the ledge and peered over.

His eyes widened in surprise. The arroyo, which should have been lush with grass from the spring rains, was trampled, the grass eaten down to the ground.

Someone had kept a herd of cattle in there.

There was only one way out—up the sloping end of the arroyo itself. Unless they swam the Pecos. Cattle weren't inclined to swim a river any more than they were inclined to climb a rocky slope unless driven to it.

Anger boiled in him. The deputy had been right. The cattle thieves were using his land for their staging area. But how the hell had they taken the cattle out?

Backing from the edge, he mounted and scouted the land until he found what he was looking for. An old cattle chute down in a pine thicket told of days past when some dreamer had tried to made a profitable ranch out of the rough tract.

His father had bought the land for back taxes, afraid that a shifty land developer would come along and put in a resort. Next thing they knew, his dad had told him, the Pecos would be dammed and people would be wa-

ter-skiing on it and complaining about the cattle pol-
luting it and scaring the tourists who picnicked or hiked
along its banks.

A resort might help his cash flow. He smiled. His
dad was probably turning over in his grave at the idea.

Leaving the gelding ground-hitched in a shady patch
of grass, he inspected the ground around the chute.
Pine needles littered the area, but they didn't obliter-
ate the signs of trespassing. He found a boot print,
several cow patties, which weren't all that old, and a
tire mark where a truck had backed and turned. The
rustlers were using his land.

All he had to do was figure out who they were, then
catch them in the act. He retrieved a camera from his
saddlebag and snapped several shots of the prints and
the chute.

Finished, he settled on a log in the shade and ate an
egg sandwich he prepared that morning and washed it
down with a cup of black coffee. He'd take some pictures of the arroyo, then head home and call Bill Merritt with the information.

Home reminded him of Molly. He'd left her asleep
that morning. She deserved a break.

Peace settled over him like a warm blanket. He'd
been out on the range for hours last week, not getting
in until his wife was in bed and asleep. Until last night,
he hadn't made love with her in five days.

His body stirred in memory. His wife—prim schoolteacher that she was—had gotten tipsy at the dance.
She'd declared she wasn't when he mentioned the fact
to her. Okay, she'd been very happy, he'd conceded.

She'd agreed to that. Then she had proceeded to at-
tack him in the most erotic manner. It had blown his

mind...and his control. They'd made love in one of the bedroom chairs, on the floor and finally in bed.

He'd been a little tipsy himself. Not on alcohol—he'd watched his intake carefully—but from Molly. When she'd asked him to sing to her again, he had.

"My song," she'd whispered, caressing him all over as if she couldn't get enough of touching. "Sing my song."

When he'd gotten to the part where he'd asked if she loved him, she kissed him as if there was no tomorrow.

He let out a ragged breath. He'd thought life's greatest moments had come with his daughter, and they had. However, Molly had brought her own special joy to his life. Long after Lass was grown and on her own, he would have Molly.

He liked that idea—him and Molly, growing old together. They'd have their grandkids out to the ranch for summers and holidays. With Molly, life would be good.

He trusted her as he had no other person since his father had died. He'd come to think of her as a friend. He wanted her as a woman. She seemed to like him, too.

Tossing down the rest of the coffee, he rose, repacked and mounted, eager to finish and go home so he could see his wife, and maybe make love when Lass had her nap. Remembering the photos, he headed the gelding toward the arroyo once more.

He smiled. Everything was working out—his life, his problems on the ranch. He was even willing to see what he could do to help his former father-in-law. Molly would give him a gold star when he told her that.

Arriving at the ledge, he reached back to unfasten the saddlebag and retrieve the camera. Before he could, a rattle warned him of another's presence. The gelding screamed, then reared and spun in a tight circle, lashing out with his forelegs.

Taken unawares, Sam fell backward from the saddle. When he hit the ground, pain spread through his side, his head and his shoulder. The startled snake slithered off into the safety of the rocky crevices.

The gelding, reins flapping behind him, took off. Sam watched the world grow dark and knew he was on the brink of passing out. He fought the blackness. He had to catch the gelding. Standing, he gave a piercing whistle. He clutched at air as he lost his balance and pitched over the ledge.

His last thought was of Molly. He wished he'd said the words...

Molly watched the two cowhands moving around the stable and outbuildings. She'd already fed the mustang. While it was eating, she'd laid a saddle blanket on its back. It hadn't moved a muscle.

She'd put a halter on it two weeks ago. It had accepted the bit after a few snorts and tosses of its head. Later the stallion had let her lift its hooves and check them. At the present, it had its head over the railing while it watched the men, too. Probably hoping for another bucket of feed.

She finished setting the table and removed the corn bread from the oven. Tonight she'd grilled a pork loin along with kabobs of peppers, onions and potatoes. After slicing the corn bread into wedges, she placed it in a cloth-lined basket and put it on the table.

"Where is your father?" she asked Lass, who had crawled off her blanket and was inspecting the legs of her high chair.

"Da-da."

"Right." She scooped the child into her arms and placed her in the high chair. Although Lass preferred table food, Molly prepared her a plate of baby food. "Nothing you can eat but potato tonight, my girl."

The men came in shortly thereafter. They helped themselves while Molly finished with Lass, who had four teeth now and liked to bite on the spoon.

"Did you see any signs of Sam?" She cast a worried glance at the darkening sky. She liked him home in the evening.

"No. He lit out on the gelding right after first light this morning. Didn't take the truck and trailer this time."

She gave Lass a cracker to chew on. Lass smiled and clicked her tongue, then settled down to eating.

"He went alone?" She didn't like that. Usually he and Bill worked together for a few hours each day, then Sam returned to the house and the ranch work.

"Guess so," Tom said.

Sandy, as usual, didn't say much of anything. He kept his eyes on his plate as he helped himself to butter and corn bread and another slice of meat.

Molly stifled her irritation with the men. Sam would be in when he got there. He could take care of himself.

This evening she didn't ask questions about the men's plans for the next day. They didn't volunteer their work schedule. The meal passed in an uneasy silence.

She glanced up once and caught Tom watching her. A funny sensation crawled over her back. He smiled and went back to eating. She listened for hoofbeats.

"We thought we might go to town," Tom said while rinsing and putting his plate in the dishwasher.

She nodded. They usually went to town on Saturday night. It was a big night out for cowboys from all the ranches while Friday was the entertainment night of choice for the townsfolk. She wondered briefly how the tradition got started.

After cleaning up the kitchen, she gave Lass a bath, then played and read to her until it was time for bed. Later, after getting into her pajamas, she roamed the house, lonely for Sam and unable to sleep.

Where was that man?

Sam woke to the cold ache of the night. He tested his side but didn't find any ribs sticking out. They were cracked maybe, but they weren't broken into pieces. He examined his shoulder.

A gash there, but not too bad. A trace of blood had dried to a crusty patch on his shirt. He was lucky the rattler hadn't sunk his fangs into him.

He'd live, he concluded. As a kid, he'd had a bite from a rattler. *That* had been a real pain.

His head hurt, but he didn't have any trouble focusing. No concussion. Thank God for small favors. He checked the sky.

Evening was coming on. Molly would worry.

He'd roused a couple of times during the afternoon, but he hadn't had the energy to try to make it out. Since no one had found him, he'd better make an effort to get home.

In fact, he had to get home. He had to protect his girls from the polecats who'd been hiding cattle on his land.

He knew who they were.

His mouth went dry at the thought of them at the ranch with Molly and Lass. Fear lent him strength and he pushed to his feet. He'd make it back if he had to crawl.

Setting his teeth against a groan, he climbed and clawed his way out of the arroyo. At the rim, he rested against a boulder, which was still warm from the sun. His breath rushed from him in harsh rasps of sound. He hoped the snake wasn't near.

Across the river, he could hear the lowing of cattle as they settled in for the night. Tisdale cattle. He wondered how many the rustlers had stolen so far.

Rising, he opened a button on his shirt and slipped his left hand inside. It wasn't much of a sling, but it was the best he could do. He had a five-hour walk ahead of him before he'd get home to his family.

His girls. Molly and Lass.

Molly couldn't settle. She surfed through the channels until she couldn't stand the noise. She stopped on a nature show, then muted the sound.

For a long minute, she listened to the night wind blowing around the house. Tonight it seemed especially lonesome.

Recalling last night, she felt the ready heat rush to her skin. She couldn't believe it was possible to love someone so much. She'd told him again and again during the hours before they fell asleep.

A smile briefly touched her lips. She couldn't believe Sam would actually sing to a woman, either, but he had. To her.

She hugged the memory to her. He had so many endearing traits...

A noise had her springing to her feet. No, it was just the nightly serenade from the coyotes beginning. She went into the kitchen and made a pot of tea. Going to the door, she peered into the dark.

The moon was bright and almost full, although the light was far from being as bright as day, as some folks said. Shadows lay over the land in sooty blackness. Daylight shadows were blue or lavender, sometimes purple, but not night shadows. They were stark in their absence of color.

She shivered and folded her arms across her waist. Come home, she silently demanded. Come home now.

The pickup the men owned was gone from its usual place next to the bunkhouse. A feeling of being utterly alone washed over her. Something felt wrong. She hesitated, then opened the door.

In her slippers, she silently crossed the gravel, feeling sharp edges through the soles of her shoes. She went into the bunkhouse and flipped on the light.

It was empty. Not just empty of the men, but bare. They'd taken their things with them, including their saddles, which usually hung from sawhorses in the corner.

That's what had bothered her. Their saddles had been under the tarp that covered their pickup bed. The saddle horns had formed identical humps, which she hadn't recognized at the time.

They didn't intend to return.

She ran back to the house and called Bill Merritt. No answer. She tried the sheriff's office. The dispatcher said he was on night duty and out on patrol. Molly left a voice mail for him to call her whenever he returned, no matter what time.

She put on a pot of strong coffee and dressed in jeans and a black shirt. If Sam didn't come in soon, she was going to start a search. Fear caught her by the throat.

Oh, Sam, please make it . . .

Who could she call to take care of Lass? Tiffany. No. She was forty minutes away. Lass's grandmother was closer.

She went to the phone, knowing Sam would be probably be furious with her for calling. "Elsie? This is Molly," she said when the phone was answered. "Could you come over, please? I need your help."

Elsie Tisdale arrived in less than thirty minutes. Her husband drove her over. "What's happened?" he asked.

"Sam hasn't come home. I'm worried about him." She offered them coffee and refilled her own cup. "I'm going to try Bill again and see if he's in."

She left another voice mail for the deputy, reminding him to call as soon as he came in. She knew the sheriff wouldn't mount a search without evidence of something wrong until Sam had been gone for twenty-four hours. She doubted a gut feeling would be considered valid evidence.

"It's only a little after nine," William Tisdale noted, glancing at the kitchen clock. "Or does he keep banker's hours?"

She rounded on him. "I don't want to hear that kind of talk. If you don't have anything important to say, then keep it to yourself. I invited Elsie here in case I decide to go look for Sam or have to take him to the hospital when I find him. You can leave at any time."

Mr. Tisdale's eyes widened at the reprimand. A flush colored his face. Molly didn't care if she'd made him angry. She was damn angry herself.

"Why do you think something's wrong?" Elsie asked. She took a seat at the table and cupped her hands around the warm mug.

"The hands have left. Cleared out," she clarified. "I think they were the ones behind the rustling. If Sam caught them, he could have been hurt."

Her imagination provided pictures of him lying alone and bleeding someplace where they would never think to look. He could be dead . . .

No, not Sam. He was too vital, too dear to her heart. She couldn't lose him. Their marriage had hardly begun.

"He can't be dead," she repeated in a hoarse whisper.

Mr. Tisdale sank heavily into a chair. He licked his lips, opened his mouth, closed it, then tried again. "It's my fault. If he's dead, it's my fault."

"Were you in with the rustlers . . . with Tom and Sandy?" It hurt to say their names. She had trusted them. Tom had kept Lass for them the night before. Surely they weren't guilty.

So why would they leave without a word of farewell?

They hadn't looked at her at supper. They'd been silent. She'd thought the tension was from her, because of Sam. Now she thought they had contributed. They must have known Sam wasn't coming in. Oh, dear God . . .

"No," Mr. Tisdale answered her. "But I started it. I paid one of my men to spread the rumors about Sam."

"Why?" she asked. Her voice shook, she was so angry. She reined her emotions in. "Why do you want to ruin him?"

"Because he had everything and I had nothing. He'd saved his money and paid off the mortgage on his ranch. We're going to lose the land." He raised haunted eyes to her. "Land that's been in my family for generations."

"So has Sam's." She refused to heed the pity that formed in her. People made choices. They had to live with the results.

"Yes. I hated it that he could come back, take over and pull this place out of the fire. I was losing out no matter what I did. I thought he would help me, but he refused. I thought, when he and Elise married, he'd be like a son, but he wasn't."

Molly stared at the older man. He seemed to be talking to himself, and the voice was one of defeat. He was giving up...on his ranch...on life...

"Sam would have helped," she said, totally certain in her estimation of her husband, "if you'd been honest with him. You tried to make it sound as if you were doing him a favor. He knew you weren't. Trust has to be earned."

He nodded his head. Elsie reached out and touched her husband's hand, lying idle on the table. She looked at him in sorrow. Molly spared a moment's pity for both of them. They'd made a lot of mistakes.

She paced to the window. Across the meadow she saw a horse silhouetted in the moonlight. It walked toward the stable. She realized something was on its back. A saddle, perhaps. No, larger than that. A man, lying over the horse's neck.

She rushed outside to meet the gelding at the paddock gate.

The big roan stopped by Molly and nuzzled her shoulder. He seemed to be asking for help. On his back, Sam clutched a handful of mane as if it were a lifeline.

"Sam, can you hear me?" she asked, laying a hand on his shoulder. She felt the dampness on his shirt and rubbed her fingers together. Sniffing, she detected the salty tang of blood. Her heart lurched painfully and started pounding.

"Molly," he gasped. "Watch out. Rustlers ... here."

"They've gone," she assured him, her tone dry. "They took off right after supper. Can you get down?"

He slid from the gelding with a groan of pain. She put her arms around him and held him upright.

"I'm all right. Let's get to the house."

"Hold on to me," she ordered, fearing he'd topple over.

"Yes, darling," he said meekly.

Relief made her dizzy. "Now I know you're going to be all right. You're making fun of me."

She guided him across the gravel driveway to the back door. Elsie held the door open for them and closed it after they were safely inside. Mr. Tisdale was on the phone.

"I don't give a damn if he's entertaining the president. I want to talk to the sheriff. Where is he?"

Molly guessed he was trying to rouse the sheriff into going after the two thieves. She led Sam down the hall to their room.

After he was seated on the chair, she unfastened his shirt and examined him. There was a bloody slash along the fleshy part of his shoulder.

"What caused this?" she asked.

"Snake," he said, grimacing as she probed the spot. "I fell off my horse." He explained briefly.

"The skin is torn." The anger burned as keen-edged as a sword in her. Because of the rustling, her man had been hurt, and she wasn't going to forget it. "The wound looks clean."

"Yeah. Help me get out of these clothes. I need a shower. Then you can bandage it," he added at her protest.

"We have to get you to the hospital. You might need a couple of stitches."

"I think we have some butterfly bandages." He gestured toward his feet. "Help me with these boots."

She pulled them off as gently as she could. She saw bruises along his side. "You're black-and-blue."

He quirked a sardonic grin her way. "Yeah, living color." He pushed to his feet and tried to unfasten his jeans with one hand. "I was lucky to catch up with the gelding later. He'd stayed close. Where are the hands?"

"Gone," she informed him. "They lit out after supper with all their gear."

"Good. I won't have to shoot them."

"You knew it was them?"

"Suspected it when you found those tire marks. Today I found the place where they worked."

"Here, let me." She pulled the snap and tugged the zipper down. "I trusted them. Tom stayed with Lass. She loved him."

"Yeah, well, just goes to show you—you can't trust your best friend nowadays."

"Why did they hang around here until after supper? They must have known you knew about them. Why didn't they take off as soon as they got back to the house?"

"They didn't want to arouse your suspicions, I assume. Maybe they were waiting to see if I'd caught on, then chickened out and decided to leave. Maybe they wanted your company and a home-cooked meal one more time. Tom was sweet on you and Lass." He smiled as if he found the idea amusing.

"I know," she said sadly. After pushing the pants down, she told him to step out.

He did, laying one hand on her head for balance. "I'll have to watch you. Always trying to get a man out of his pants."

She looked up at him. Something in his eyes gave her pause. She shook her head. He was hurt and vulnerable right now. What she saw was gratitude for her help.

"I'll get the shower started." She dashed into the bathroom and adjusted the spray to a comfortable warmth.

Sam followed her. He'd finished undressing. A sigh escaped him when he stepped under the water.

"Wait. I'll come in with you." She stripped as quickly as she could and stepped into the shower.

Sam leaned against the tile wall, his eyes closed. He looked so utterly weary. A wave of tenderness washed over her with the cascading of the water down her back. Along with it grew a fierce protective anger on his behalf.

Soaping her hands, she washed him carefully, checking his body for scrapes and bruises as she did. Other than the graze on his shoulder and the bruise on his side, he didn't appear to have any other injuries.

She found the bump on his head when she washed his hair. The anger rekindled.

Sam touched the frown lines between her eyes. "Don't look so fierce. You make me nervous."

"It makes me angry that you were hurt."

"Make me feel better," he suggested. He pulled her against him and kissed her.

The passion surprised her. "You . . . we can't," she whispered when he kissed down her neck. "The Tisdales are here. You're injured." Otherwise, she'd have taken everything he offered.

He gave a brief laugh. "Don't I know it. But I'm not dead. Tomorrow I'll be as good as new. Right now, you'd better get me to bed before I fall on my face."

She dried him off, then wrapped a towel around her and led him to bed. She rubbed antibiotic ointment on his wound and taped a gauze square over it. He ran a finger along her skin just above the towel. "Stop that," she ordered, smiling.

After tucking him in, she dressed again, combed her hair and, after checking him one more time, headed for the kitchen.

Bill Merritt had arrived. "Tisdale told me an interesting tale. He thinks your ranch hands saw the main chance when he spread the rumors about Sam rustling cattle. They decided to make the story true, thinking they'd get the benefit and Sam would get the blame."

She sank into a chair and pushed her damp hair back from her face. "It looks that way. They left tonight with all their gear in their truck, so I don't guess they mean to come back."

"How's Sam? What happened to him?"

She repeated the story she'd pieced together while she'd washed her husband and taken care of his injuries.

"A rattlesnake?" Bill whistled at her nod. "He's lucky to be alive. By the way, we have an all-points bulletin out on the pickup, also your cattle truck."

She looked questioningly at him.

"It's missing. I figure one of them is driving it, loaded with the cattle they stole. If it's spotted, we want to follow them and see who's buying."

"Catch the source, huh?" Tisdale chipped in. He looked pretty grim.

Molly glanced at the clock. After eleven.

Elsie followed her gaze. "I suppose there's nothing more we can do tonight. It's time we were getting home." She stood and looked expectantly at her husband.

William seemed startled by her decisive manner.

To Molly, Elsie seemed younger and more energetic than when they'd first met. Tonight she'd dressed in blue slacks and a white shirt with a blue scarf around her neck. She wore sapphires in her ears and a matching ring on her right hand.

Perhaps the woman had recovered her spirit. Love could do that to a person, and Elsie certainly loved Lass.

"We'll need a statement from you," Bill told the older man, "on your part in all this."

Tisdale started to argue, then stopped at a look from Elsie. "I'll come down to the station tomorrow."

"Some of your men might be involved," the deputy went on, thinking aloud about the case. "We'll have to check that out."

Again William appeared to want to argue. He heaved a deep breath, his mouth settling into grim lines. He may have been handsome once, but now he looked tired and frayed around the edges. His anger at Sam had disappeared in the face of the problems he'd caused. She wondered if he'd be arrested as the instigator of the crime.

Molly walked them to the door. She kissed Elsie's cheek. "Thank you for coming."

"I'd like to come back. Anytime you need a babysitter, I'm only a phone call away. I hope you'll let me."

"Of course." She looked at Mr. Tisdale. "Thank you for coming tonight."

He flushed. "I'm a damn fool," he said. "You can tell Sam I said that."

She smiled. "You can count on it."

After they left, Bill lingered while he drank the coffee. He had until midnight before he was off duty. Molly politely kept him company, but she wished he'd leave. She wanted to go to her husband.

"Well, one thing for sure—Sam won't have to worry about his father-in-law anymore," Bill commented.

"Do you think he's seen the error of his ways?"

"I don't know about that, but when this comes out, Tisdale will be ruined in this community. Sam's name will be cleared."

Chapter Thirteen

Molly woke the next morning to a loud banging. She sat straight up in bed and looked around wildly.

"Someone's at the door," Sam said, pushing the covers back. "I hope they have a damn good reason for waking us up." He groaned when he rose from the bed.

She noted the bruise on his side had spread roughly into the size of a soccer ball. "You're lucky you didn't break something when you fell."

"Yeah, good thing I took most of the fall on my head."

She grimaced at his levity. He treated his injuries lightly because of her, she suspected.

The banging rattled through the house.

"Coming," Sam yelled.

"They'll wake up Lass," she grumbled, pulling on her robe and slippers. She pulled a comb through her hair and washed her face, then helped Sam with a pair of jeans and a shirt, then shoes and socks.

He followed her to the kitchen.

They could see the shape of a man silhouetted against the dawn on the other side of the door. Sam went over and opened it.

"Good morning. You out for a snipe hunt?" he asked with dry humor when Bill Merritt stepped inside.

"Morning, Sam, Molly," the deputy said.

Molly, busy putting on a pot of coffee, returned his greeting. "What *are* you doing out at five o'clock?"

"We got your rustlers."

"Tom and Sandy? Where'd you catch them?" Sam asked.

"Down by your stable."

Molly whipped around and stared at the deputy. "Here? On our place? Had they come back for more cattle?"

"No. They were returning the truck they'd borrowed." Bill nodded toward the outdoors. "I've got a man on them."

"Now?" Molly couldn't believe the two cowboys would have the nerve to show up on the ranch.

"Yeah. Turns out they weren't rustling."

"How do you figure that?" Sam eased down in a chair at the table and motioned the deputy to a seat.

Molly brought coffee to the table and poured them each a mug before she started breakfast.

"According to their story, they borrowed the truck to transport their cattle to their place about a hundred miles from here. My man picked up on the truck license when they were on their way back and called me. I told him to follow and keep me posted. When I realized they were heading this way, I came on over to see what was happening." His eyes gleamed with amusement. "They filled your tank with gas when they came through town. Thoughtful crooks, huh?"

Sam snorted. "How about bringing them in and let's see if we can get to the bottom of this?"

Bill went outside. In a minute, he returned with the two culprits behind him. The other cop took up a guard position on the porch. The cowboys took their hats off and stood in the middle of the room, shuffling from foot to foot.

"You may as well sit down," Sam advised.

Molly cooked a pound of bacon, then started the pancakes. She set mugs out for the two rustlers and poured coffee for them.

"You boys want to tell me your story before I shoot you?" Sam asked cordially.

Molly gave him a startled glance.

The two men looked at each other, then Tom started. "We weren't stealing. Those cows belonged to us, free and clear."

"Yeah," Sandy asserted.

"How do you figure that?"

"We found 'em. They were range cattle."

"No brands?" Sam asked. He studied the two men while he sipped the hot coffee.

"That's right," Tom said while Sandy nodded vigorously.

Sam peered at Bill. Bill shrugged. "I have a man checking it out."

"If they were range cattle, why'd you hide them and make off in the middle of the night?" Sam demanded.

An uncomfortable silence ensued. Finally Tom burst out, "We didn't want you to steal 'em from us."

Sam's eyebrows rose at this statement. He shook his head slightly when Molly would have pounced on the ridiculous claim.

"Why would I do that?"

"Our last boss did." With that, the two men braced themselves as if expecting to have to fight their way out of the kitchen. They watched Sam warily.

"Hmm." Sam turned sideways, grimacing as he did and placing a hand against his sore ribs. He straightened his legs. "I guess you're going to have to help me out. You'd collected a herd of range cattle, but your boss stole them from you?"

"He said they were his, that we found 'em on his property. That was a lie. We didn't. We rounded them up in our spare time on open range and moved them to a pen. That was the deal."

Sandy broke in. "We worked for less wages so we'd have time to start our own herd. We were supposed to have the use of a pasture to keep them in until we had enough to move them to our place. He threatened to have us arrested for rustling if we took one cow off his land."

"Ah," Sam said.

Molly brought plates and silverware to the table. "Sit still," she told Bill when he started to rise. "You might as well eat, too. Unless you've had breakfast?"

"No, ma'am." He sniffed loudly. "That sure smells good."

"Tell your assistant to come in," she suggested. "He's probably hungry, too."

Bill called the man in. She put syrup and pancakes and bacon on the table, then replenished the coffee mugs and took her place by Sam.

She smiled happily. "This looks like a family meal."

"I'm gonna miss your cooking, Molly," Tom said with a great deal of sorrow in his voice.

"Why is that?" Sam asked. "Are you going to do your own cooking at the bunkhouse?"

Tom and Sandy looked at him, puzzlement appearing on their forlorn faces.

"It takes money to start a ranching operation," he continued thoughtfully. "You might want to keep up your jobs here... unless you have a big hunk of savings."

Bill poured a pond of syrup over his stack of pancakes. "I take it you're not going to press charges?"

"No." Sam poured an equal amount of syrup over his stack. "No law against moving your own cattle, is there?"

"No, but what about the truck?"

"Tom is the *segundo*. You give Sandy permission to borrow the truck?" he asked his new foreman.

Tom nodded slowly. He looked as if he were dreaming and was afraid he might wake up at any second.

"There," Sam said to Bill, "he had permission."

"Well, hell, it seems I got out of bed at four for nothing. And I have the midnight shift again tonight. I ought to charge you for my overtime," he told Sam before forking a big bite of pancake into his mouth.

Sam merely grinned.

The other deputy laughed. Molly did, too, then she leaned over and kissed Sam's check.

"Mmm," he murmured, "what was that for?"

"For being wonderful. Lass would never have forgiven you if you'd driven Tom away, and Porsche has a weakness for Sandy. He lets her sleep with her head in his boot at night."

"That probably works better than a flea collar," Sam mused.

That produced guffaws from everyone but Sandy, who turned a brilliant shade of red.

Molly ate her breakfast, her heart at ease about their two cowhands. She and Lass had come to love them. "But what about the other rancher?" she asked, recalling the wounded man. "Did you shoot him when he found you?"

"That weren't us." Tom shook his head vehemently. "Me and Sandy, we didn't do no shooting and we weren't on anybody's property but ours, yours and the open range."

"Then who did it?"

"Real rustlers," Bill told them. "We've been keeping more than one outfit under surveillance this week. They were using old homesteads around here to hold stolen stock until they could get them moved. The state police caught up with them last night. That's where I was when you called, Molly, helping out on a stakeout and arrest."

"Oh. So you knew Tom and Sandy weren't part of it."

"Well, I knew they weren't part of that gang, but I assumed they had a scam of their own going."

"All's well that ends well," she murmured with a glad smile at Tom and Sandy. Her faith in them had been restored. She heard Lass cry out. "There's our girl. I'll get her."

She went to the bedroom. Lass was standing up in the crib, looking like a prisoner planning an escape. "Hello, darling," she said, bustling around the room.

After opening the blinds, she washed the baby's face, then dressed her in rompers and warm socks with grippers on the bottom. "Ma-ma," Lass said.

Molly paused, then finished fastening the snaps on the rompers. "Let's go see Daddy and Tom and Sandy."

"Da-da." Lass patted Molly's cheek as they entered the kitchen. "Ma-ma."

Molly quickly looked at Sam. His gaze flicked to hers, but she couldn't tell what he was thinking. Would he mind if Lass called her *Mother?*

She'd better ask before it became ingrained with the child. So far she'd referred to herself as Molly, but she wanted Lass to call her mother. It seemed natural and right to her.

After setting Lass in the high chair, she spooned cereal and fruit into the rosebud mouth, feeling very maternal with the eyes of the men on her.

Bill sighed and rose. "Time to go," he told his assistant. "We need to get some sleep. No telling what adventures we'll have in this crime-ridden county tonight." Chuckling he and the other officer left.

Tom and Sandy stood, too. "Do we really have a job here for the rest of the summer?" Tom asked.

"If you want it."

The men looked at each other, then at Sam. "We sure do." They picked up their hats and headed out.

"Well, that leaves us," he said when they were alone.

"Yes," she said, spooning the last bite into Lass's mouth. "I have a plan to help the Tisdales," she told him and waited to see if he would explode in anger.

"Now why doesn't that surprise me?" he murmured, watching her with a pensive look in his eyes.

She couldn't tell if he was angry or not. "Do you want to hear it?"

"Oh, yes. Please, continue."

"Well, I have a thousand shares of stock my grandmother gave me. I thought I'd sell part of it. I'll invest the money in the Tisdale land and combine it with ours. They could live there as long as they want. What do you think?"

He studied her for a long minute. "How much is that stock worth?"

"About a million."

"Dollars?"

"Yes." She wiped Lass's face with a damp cloth and put her in the playpen. Picking up her cup, she took a drink, then turned to face Sam. "You look sort of funny," she said. "Are you coming down with something?"

He pushed himself to his feet. "Why didn't you tell me?" he asked, his voice quiet and devoid of expression.

"Tell you what?"

"About the money. People thought you were a good catch before, now they'll be sure I married you because of it."

"So what?" she said, not seeing the problem he evidently did. "We'll know better."

"Do you?"

She smiled across the table at him. "Of course. You're way too smart to marry someone for money."

He walked across the room and out the door.

She went after him. "It isn't polite to walk out on someone in the midst of a quarrel," she informed him. Not that she was angry, but he seemed troubled. "If we have a difference, it's better to air the problem than let it fester.''

"Later," he said. "We'll talk later." He headed for the barn while she stared at his back.

Sam leaned on the fence and watched the stallion. The big horse eyed him, its ears twitching back and forth. Slowly it crossed the paddock and came to him. It sniffed a time or two, then nuzzled his shirt, probably catching Molly's scent on him.

He moved back a step so the stallion wouldn't nudge his sore shoulder while it searched for Molly.

A million dollars. He hadn't guessed. Stupid. The signs had been there. The sophistication of her parents. Her brother who had argued cases in front of the Supreme Court. Her grandmother who was off on a world tour or something like that. Molly's education in a private girl's academy. Her degrees from an Ivy League university. He should have known.

A million dollars. He'd have to think about that. Would a woman like her really want to stay with a man like him? He couldn't give her a mansion or a fancy car. He didn't need to. She could buy all that for herself.

He pressed a hand over his eyes, thinking of her cooking for him and the hands. She'd washed his clothes and lectured him on hanging up his damp towels. How long would she be content playing the rancher's wife?

Six months. He'd give her six months. Then she'd be tired of him and want to be free.

For a moment, he considered trying to hold her with sex, with the child she thought she wanted. But he wouldn't do that.

The knowledge sat heavily on his shoulders as he went to check the calves in the barn. Tom and Sandy had finished the chores. Now they were restoring their possessions in the bunkhouse and discussing plans for the future.

It wasn't fair—to be handed a slice of paradise and have it jerked away before he'd gotten more than a taste. No matter. He'd have to do whatever was fair to Molly.

Right now she had the idea she wanted to buy a ranch. He'd have to talk her out of that. Her money was safer where it was.

He'd talk to his former in-laws and see what he could do for them. William might be arrested as an instigator of the rustling incidents that had happened recently. The ringleader had been the man he'd paid to start the rumors, according to the deputy.

He gripped the railing and stared at the sky, the rancher part of him noting the clouds blowing before the wind. They'd have a storm that night.

"Here, hold Lass," Molly told him, stopping by the fence.

He hadn't heard her approach. His heart squeezed into a tight ball of longing. He recognized the symptom.

Fool that he was, he'd fallen in love with his wife.

He couldn't say the words. If he told her now, she'd think it was because of the money, even though she said she didn't. He knew how people's minds worked. If a man's own mother hadn't believed him, why would anyone else?

Lass patted his cheek and tried to hold on to his nose. "Da-da," she said, giving him her biggest grin.

He rubbed his cheek on her soft curls while Molly went into the stable. She called the stallion by banging a pail against a post. The stallion headed for the open door.

Inside Sam could hear Molly talking to the horse, calling him pet names and laughing when he tried to nuzzle her. The stallion liked to snuffle along her neck. Sam thought the horse liked the scent of Molly's soap.

"Here I come, ready or not," she called.

Before he had time to think what this meant, Molly came out of the stable. She was riding the stallion.

Sam went utterly still. Fear beat its way to his throat and lodged there. "Molly, be careful," he said softly, trying not to show his worry.

"It's okay. I've been riding him for a week. I wanted to surprise you."

"You have," he told her, "in more ways than one."

"Can we keep him? Perhaps for a stud?"

"He's your horse. You can do whatever you want with him."

"Oh, Sam, really? He's mine?"

He nodded, then swallowed hard. She looked as if he'd given her the moon. Would she be as thrilled with his love?

She'd said she loved him, but sex could make a person think that. It was so good between them . . . The heat began to pump through him. He tried to turn the thoughts off.

"Watch," she called. She rode the mustang around the paddock in a circle, then she had him back up. "That's all I've taught him so far. I haven't taken him outside yet. I was afraid he'd head for the hills." She grinned.

"Ma-ma," Lass said and waved at Molly. "Ma-ma."

Molly glanced at him, then away. The mustang was acting up, prancing and shying at imaginary enemies. She had her hands full trying to rein him in.

"He needs a good run," Sam called to her. "Do you want to take him out in the pasture?"

She nodded.

He went around and opened the gate, then stood behind it while she coaxed the mustang outside. The stallion was suspicious of this sudden freedom.

Molly clicked at him and urged him forward. He broke into a canter, then swung into a loping run. Molly stretched out over his neck, her hair blowing wildly. Sam heard her laughter as they bounded away.

Going to the porch, he sat on the steps with Lass and watched the horse and rider. Molly was everything he wanted in a woman—an enthusiastic lover, a sympathetic companion, a loving mother, an accomplished rider, teacher, citizen. And friend.

How long before she tired of ranch life?

Molly brushed the tangle of hair back from her temples. The ride had been exhilarating. The mustang was calm, his excess energy spent. He looked around with a keen eye, interested in everything on the ranch. An intelligent animal.

She smiled with pride when she rode back into the paddock and waved at Sam. Lass was crawling on the porch, inspecting everything she came across. He hadn't said anything when the baby had called her Mama.

Wanting to be with them, she hurriedly dismounted and put the gear away, then brushed the stallion until he was dry. She left him with a bucket of feed in his stall.

After washing up at the utility sink in the stable, she and the cats joined the other two on the porch. Porsche jumped to the railing and settled into a ball of contentment. Persnickety rubbed against Lass and purred loudly when Lass grabbed a handful of fur.

Molly settled beside Sam with a happy sigh. "That was fun, but I might not be able to climb out of bed tomorrow. It's been years since I've ridden like that."

"You're good. You must have had a horse when you were a kid." There was a question in his voice.

She shook her head. "Summer camps."

"Oh, of course." His tone was sardonic.

"We need to talk, I think," she said. "Why does it bother you that I have money?"

"It doesn't."

She searched his eyes, wondering at the darkness of his mood. "I can't figure you out. You should be happy that the rustling has been solved and our men cleared, yet something is eating at you. If it's not the money, then what is it?"

"It's nothing." He gave her a half smile filled with irony. "Just a little quandary of my own."

He wasn't going to tell her. Disappointment bit into her. She'd thought they were growing close. She was obviously mistaken. Well, she'd been wrong before.

She studied her silent husband with quick glances at his face. He grimaced when he reached over to collect Lass, who was peering at a mesquite branch hanging over the railing.

"Poor darling," she murmured, remembering his injuries.

He was tired and out of sorts and probably aching all over. Neither of them had had a great deal of sleep last night.

She ran her fingers up and down his back. "Why don't you take a nap?" she suggested. "Lass will want one after she has her bottle, so the house should be quiet."

"That sounds good." He didn't look at her or take notice of her caresses.

Remembering how he'd embraced her during the shower, she tried to figure out his change in mood. Surely money couldn't make that much difference to him. It wasn't as if she'd lied. She'd listed all her assets in the prenuptial agreement.

"It wasn't my fault if you didn't realize the thousand shares were worth a lot," she said aloud.

He stiffened. "I realize that."

"So why should it make any difference now?"

"It doesn't."

"Good." Springing up, she lifted Lass and took her inside. She warmed a bottle and, going to the nursery, sat in the recliner rocker and fed Lass the formula.

The child gazed up at her, one plump hand patting the bottle while she drank.

"Your father is a hard man to figure out," she told her.

Lass stopped sucking and grinned up at her. Molly's heart contracted with love. She couldn't imagine being anywhere but here, in this house, with this family.

But what if Sam didn't want her?

Now that he was clear of all threats from his father-in-law, he no longer needed to worry about anyone taking Lass from him. Certainly he didn't need a spinsterish teacher who lectured on everything from table manners to bath towels in his life.

As Lass's eyes drooped, then closed in sleep, Molly wrestled with the problem of understanding her husband. Well, she'd take it one day at a time and see what developed. She grimaced at her own optimistic attitude. Molly, the great philosopher.

After laying Lass down, she went to the master bedroom. Sam was there. He'd undressed to his briefs and was lying under the sheet, one arm over his face.

She stripped to her underwear and joined him.

To her surprise, he rolled toward her and laid his arm over her waist. She turned to her side and snuggled into his body, spoon-fashion. His breath sighed against her hair, then deepened. She realized he was asleep.

For a few moments, she pondered the way he'd looked at her yesterday when he arrived home and found out she and the baby were all right. It had been fierce, yet tender. She'd thought it was because he was injured and vulnerable, but maybe... maybe she was wrong...

Molly and Lass stood at the window and waved one last time. Nana waved from the window of the plane. The plane moved away from the gate. Behind them, Sam waited silently to drive them back to the ranch.

"I hate to see her go, but truthfully, I'm exhausted," Molly admitted, heaving a sigh of part sadness, part weariness.

"Your grandmother is an energetic lady," he commented, taking Lass from her and guiding them toward the door.

"Fortunately she doesn't stay in one place longer than ten days, as a rule. She says that's the limit of her patience. I think that's all ordinary people can last with her."

During the past ten days, they'd made a thorough tour of the area, looking at landmarks, ghost towns, museums and meeting all the local citizens. The last thing Nana had whispered to her was, "He's a keeper, your young man. Makes me miss my Bertie."

Molly blinked away the mist from her eyes. "We'd better hurry. Chuck and Janice will be at the house before we get back. I'd like to have a leisurely dinner with them before the Tisdales arrive to discuss the legalities."

The two ranches were forming a joint project where their land met at the river. They were going to open a limited area to wilderness camping for families, plus a youth work camp for city kids to build trails, clear brush from campsites and learn to ride and herd cattle and get paid for it.

They arrived at the ranch five minutes before their dinner guests. The other couple pitched in. Soon the meal was on the table. Afterward, they went into the living room and discussed the project over coffee while waiting for the older couple.

"You sure you want to do this?" Chuck asked.

Sam glanced at Molly, smiled and nodded.

Chuck perused one, then the other. He started laughing.

"What's so funny?" his wife demanded. She smoothed her maternity smock over her rounded tummy.

"I gave Sam some advice once. He wasn't sure it was the best advice, but he took it."

"What was the advice?" Janice asked.

"How about another cup of coffee?" Sam interrupted, springing to his feet.

Molly looked from one man to the other. "I detect a devious plot here, Janice. Do you?"

"Absolutely. We'll tickle you to death if you don't tell us right now."

Chuck nodded to Sam. "It's his secret. Shall I tell?"

Sam refilled their cups and replaced the pot on the tray. He shrugged. "Why not? They'll bug us from now until eternity or until they find out, whichever comes first."

"I advised Sam to marry the nursery schoolteacher as a way to solve his problems with his former father-in-law."

Molly's smile retreated. She pushed it back on her face.

"Told him it was my best advice. And it was." Chuck beamed at them, quite pleased with his legal counseling.

"Yeah, it was," Sam agreed.

A beat of silence followed while he gazed at Molly. She felt the tenderness of his look and swallowed against the emotion that closed her throat.

Marriage was good, she mused as the conversation flowed around her. She and Sam had a solid relationship. Tomorrow, they would have made it six months. Six months of marriage to a man she loved more than anything. She sighed. Yes, it was good.

The Tisdales arrived, and the talk grew lively. There had been times during the past months when she and Elsie had had to intervene between the two strong-minded men.

Moving around the kitchen, cutting the pie and serving dessert, she wondered if anyone noticed she always included food during their meetings. The ritual stemmed from ancient times.

Sitting down to a feast symbolized peace and a measure of trust between two warring factions. Only the lowest form of humanity would betray this sacred treaty. She'd found it worked as well in modern times.

William had shed his anger slowly, like a snake shuffling off its old skin. It had been interesting to watch the transformation. Gradually the charming man he had once been had emerged from the twin shadows of resentment and frustration.

As for Elsie... Molly studied her friend while she placed the plates on the table. Elsie was positively blooming under the gentle warmth of Lass's love.

Yes, life was good. Tomorrow, on the day of their six-month anniversary, she had a favor to ask of Sam. A hint of the nervousness she felt deep inside penetrated her poise.

She would soon be thirty-three. It was time.

Chapter Fourteen

The day had been hot for October, but now the shadows were long under the mesquite branches, and the air had cooled. Molly smiled as Lass followed the cat around the porch.

The "yearling," as Sam had called her since her birthday, walked with that all-out gait toddlers used to get from one place to another, her eyes always on the prize she was after and never on her feet. She wore sneakers—her first pair of real shoes and a gift from Elsie.

Across the pasture, she could see Sam and the two cowhands pulling barbed wire tight and stapling it to posts. They were moving the cattle in close for the winter. During the summer the field had grown alfalfa, now stored in a huge barn as hay.

She'd planned a special supper for the men. Chicken-fried steak and mashed potatoes, with gravy smothering everything. Also baking powder biscuits, which she'd learned to make just right by trial and error.

She grinned. Terrible tastes these Western men had, but once a month she indulged it. She had grown to like gravy and biscuits herself.

Nana, who was originally from the South, had laughed about that. "You'll make a cowgirl out of her yet," she'd said to Sam.

"I hope so," he'd replied, giving Molly one of those mysterious glances that stopped her heart. If only Western men weren't so darn silent!

When the men headed in, she set the table and had their supper laid out by the time they came to the house.

"Next year, I'd like a garden," she said, taking her place beside Lass. She'd found it was easier to sit beside Sam with Lass in the high chair between them at the corner of the table.

Sam paused as if studying the idea from every angle. "It's a lot of work," he finally said.

"I know, but I'd like to try it one time. Maybe Mrs. Stevens would come more often."

"We could plow it for you," Tom volunteered. He paused. "Uh, if we're here next year."

"You'd better be," Sam ordered. "You'll have most of the responsibility for the ranch while the resort is getting off the ground. If it does."

Molly grinned at his skepticism. "It'll be fun. We'll use camp hosts like the National Park Service does to keep an eye on the campers and report any problems."

"We'll probably spend half our time rescuing lost kids." Sam smiled when she started laughing. "All right, I'll quit being such a pessimist."

When dinner was over, he gave Lass a bath and got her ready for bed while Molly cleaned the kitchen. She listened with a deep inner contentment to Lass's shouts of glee as she splashed in the tub. Sam's deeper rumble scored a vibrant counterpoint to the child's treble tones.

She hummed while she finished up. After a while, feeling another presence, she looked up. Sam lounged against the doorframe, watching her work. She smiled at him.

"Lass is ready for her story," he said.

She rubbed lotion into her hands and went to the bedroom. Holding the child in her lap, she read a bedtime story about some bears going into the woods at night. Lass pointed to the pictures and growled in imitation of her father.

"That's right. The bears go *grrrr,*" Molly agreed.

Once again Sam watched from the door with an unreadable expression in his eyes. A shiver sluiced down Molly's back. There'd been such a depth of emotion in his glances of late. She couldn't figure out if it forebode trouble or not.

After Lass was settled with her blanket and a thumb in her mouth, Molly slipped out of the room and closed the door.

Going to the master bedroom, she found Sam in the sitting room, which doubled as the ranch office, watching the news on television. He'd showered and put on a blue sweat suit.

Her heart skipped, then settled down. She flew into the shower and out again in five minutes, eager to be with her husband. They still made love nearly every night, but Saturday night was their "date" night.

After blow-drying her hair, she added cologne at a few strategic locations and slipped into a new nightgown frothy with lace and the color of champagne. With the robe, she was modestly covered, but everything about the outfit whispered "seduction."

That's exactly what she meant to do.

She glided into the sitting room in her bare feet and sat beside Sam on the daybed, curling her body toward his and resting her legs across his.

"You smell good," he said, dropping an arm around her shoulders. He rubbed a smoothly shaven jaw against her head.

"You do, too." She took a breath. "Sam—"

"Molly—"

They stopped and looked at each other expectantly.

"Ladies first," he offered.

"No. You." She was about to chicken out.

He nodded. He reached behind him and pulled a box from under a pillow. "For our six-month anniversary."

"Oh, Sam," she whispered, touched that he'd noted the date. The box contained a necklace and earrings that matched her engagement ring. "Oh, how beautiful. I can't imagine a more perfect gift."

"I can," he murmured.

She looked up. Her gaze was trapped by his.

"I watched you and Lass tonight. She's your daughter in every way that counts. I thought...I wondered if you'd be willing to make it legal."

"Adopt her?" Her heart soared like a helium balloon. "Of course I will. I've thought about it, but I wasn't sure...I didn't want you to think I was pushing...Oh, Sam, you know how much I love her." She set the box on the table and kissed him rapturously all over his smiling face.

He chuckled and caught her mouth in a shattering kiss. She sighed and laid her head on his chest when it ended. His heart was pounding hard. Against her thigh, she felt the arousal that always followed their kisses. That reminded her...

"I have a request," she murmured, no longer shy about asking for her favor.

"Ask away." He idly smoothed her hair.

"Could we start a baby now, tonight?"

She felt him stiffen and wondered if she'd read the situation wrong. She lifted her head and gazed at him.

Time stopped, just stopped, and lingered suspended in the dark blaze of his eyes for an eternity.

"Sam?" she said and heard her voice tremble.

He didn't speak. She suspected he couldn't. She saw him swallow, then take a deep breath. His heart knocked against her breasts in a pagan beat that started an answering beat in her.

She didn't need the words. She saw it in his eyes—the love he couldn't, didn't try to hide, the fierce protective love that was utterly sweet and utterly tender.

This time it was for her.

"Sam, my love." She raised her face, needing his kiss.

He kissed her lips, her cheek, her ear. Then he said the words. "Molly... I love you."

So softly. A whisper of sound. Words. Tender. Loving.

Words. For her.

"You're the only woman I've ever loved, truly loved."

She couldn't believe it was possible for one body to hold so much happiness. "I believe you."

Laughing, Sam lifted her into his arms and carried her to their bed. He laid her down as if she was precious. To him, she was ... this woman who believed in him, who'd taken his part and kept faith with him, who'd made each day a joy and showed him in a thousand ways that she was in for the long haul ... this woman who loved him and Lass with a deep, abiding love that they'd come to trust and depend on.

Yeah, he loved her.

He gathered her close, needing to say the words in his heart. "Molly. Molly, darling."

"Love me," she said, restless for him. "Just love me."

"Forever," he promised.

And he did.

*   *   *   *   *

Now that Molly has found love, see her brother, Gareth Clelland, take the plunge!

All-business Gareth is at a loss when his assistant goes into labor at his isolated cabin—leaving him to deliver the baby! Can An Unexpected Delivery lead Gareth to a family of his own? Find out next month, when Laurie Paige presents Silhouette Romance readers with a BUNDLE OF JOY!

An Unexpected Delivery

by Laurie Paige

Silhouette Romance #1151

May 1996

Silhouette®

SPECIAL EDITION™

COMING NEXT MONTH

#1027 PART-TIME WIFE—Susan Mallery
That Special Woman!/Hometown Heartbreakers

When Jill Bradford took the position of nanny to three adorable boys, she was determined that it stay a business arrangement. But the boys' father, Craig Haynes, wanted more than just a part-time mother or wife. He wanted Jill forever.

#1028 EXPECTANT FATHER—Leanne Banks

Caleb Masters was intelligent, gorgeous—everything Glory Danson desired in a man. Becoming pregnant with his child, she married for the sake of the baby...but would the expectant father and mom-to-be find love ever after?

#1029 ON MOTHER'S DAY—Andrea Edwards
Great Expectations

When Alex Rinehart reunited Fiona Scott with the daughter she'd given up for adoption, he helped her save the child she thought she'd never see again. And now that Alex and Fiona had found each other, Fiona had more than one reason to celebrate on Mother's Day.

#1030 NEW BRIDE IN TOWN—Amy Frazier
Sweet Hope Weddings

Belle Sherman had arrived and the town of Sweet Hope—and its most eligible bachelor, Boone O'Malley—would never be the same again. When these opposites attracted, there was no stopping Belle from being the next bride in town, unless her groom got cold feet!

#1031 RAINSINGER—Ruth Wind

Daniel Lynch was a drop-dead handsome Navajo with black eyes and an attitude to match. And suddenly Winona Snow found herself sharing her house with him! Soon this stubborn man held the key to her future...and her heart.

#1032 MARRY ME, NOW!—Allison Hayes

She had to save the ranch, but first Dacy Fallon needed to convince old flame Nick Reynolds to accept her help. He wouldn't admit that the old attraction was as strong as ever, but Dacy was determined to win herself a cowboy groom....

MILLION DOLLAR SWEEPSTAKES
AND EXTRA BONUS PRIZE DRAWING

As seen on TV!
Free Gift Offer

With a Free Gift proof-of-purchase from any Silhouette® book,
you can receive a beautiful cubic zirconia pendant.

This gorgeous marquise-shaped stone is a genuine cubic
zirconia—accented by an 18" gold tone necklace.

(Approximate retail value $19.95)

Send for yours today...
compliments of  *Silhouette*®

To receive your free gift, a cubic zirconia pendant, send us one original proof-of-
purchase, photocopies not accepted, from the back of any Silhouette Romance™,
Silhouette Desire®, Silhouette Special Edition®, Silhouette Intimate Moments®
or Silhouette Shadows™ title available in February, March or April at your favorite
retail outlet, together with the Free Gift Certificate, plus a check or money order for
$1.75 U.S./$2.25 CAN. (do not send cash) to cover postage and handling, payable
to Silhouette Free Gift Offer. We will send you the specified gift. Allow 6 to 8 weeks for
delivery. Offer good until April 30, 1996 or while quantities last. Offer valid in the U.S. and
Canada only.

Free Gift Certificate

Name: _____

Address: _____

City: _____ State/Province: _____ Zip/Postal Code: _____

Mail this certificate, one proof-of-purchase and a check or money order for postage
and handling to: SILHOUETTE FREE GIFT OFFER 1996. In the U.S.: 3010 Walden
Avenue, P.O. Box 9057, Buffalo NY 14269-9057. In Canada: P.O. Box 622, Fort Erie,

---

FREE GIFT OFFER   079-KBZ-R

ONE PROOF-OF-PURCHASE

To collect your fabulous FREE GIFT, a cubic zirconia pendant, you must include this
original proof-of-purchase for each gift with the properly completed Free Gift Certificate.

You're About to Become a

Privileged Woman

Reap the rewards of fabulous free gifts and benefits with proofs-of-purchase from Silhouette and Harlequin books

Pages & Privileges™

It's our way of thanking you for buying our books at your favorite retail stores.

PROOF OF PURCHASE

SSE-PP126

Offer expires October 31, 1996

Pages & Privileges ™

Harlequin and Silhouette— the most privileged readers in the world!

For more information about Harlequin and Silhouette's PAGES & PRIVILEGES program call the Pages & Privileges Benefits Desk: 1-503-794-2499

Silhouette®